"No! There's been a terrible mistake!"

Lara cried. "Donovan didn't do it. He couldn't have."

The load on Donovan's heart lifted. She'd come. She was going to tell the truth. No matter what happened, he could live with it.

The sheriff squared his shoulders and stared at Lara. "What do you mean, he *couldn't* have?"

Lara looked directly at Donovan as she answered. "Donovan Delaney couldn't have hurt that girl last night," she said in a firm voice. "I'm his alibi."

"Beg pardon?" the sheriff asked, frowning.

Lara's chin lifted in an imperious manner that almost dared anyone to question or doubt what she was about to say. "Donovan couldn't have done that terrible thing to that girl, because he was at my house.

"In my bed."

Dear Reader,

The most wonderful time of the year just got better! These six captivating romances from Special Edition are sure to brighten your holidays.

Reader favorite Sherryl Woods is back by popular demand with the latest addition to her series AND BABY MAKES THREE: THE DELACOURTS OF TEXAS. In *The Delacourt Scandal,* a curious reporter seeking revenge unexpectedly finds love.

And just in time for the holidays, Lisa Jackson kicks off her exciting new miniseries THE McCAFFERTYS with *The McCaffertys: Thorne,* where a hero's investigation takes an interesting turn when he finds himself face-to-face with his ex-lover. Unwrap the next book in A RANCHING FAMILY, a special gift this month from Victoria Pade. In *The Cowboy's Gift-Wrapped Bride,* a Wyoming rancher is startled not only by his undeniable attraction to an amnesiac beauty he found in a blizzard, but also by the tantalizing secrets she reveals as she regains her memory.

And in RUMOR HAS IT…, a couple separated by tragedy in the past finally has a chance for love in Penny Richards's compelling romance, *Lara's Lover.* The holiday cheer continues with Allison Leigh's emotional tale of a runaway American heiress who becomes a *Mother in a Moment* after she agrees to be nanny to a passel of tots.

And silver wedding bells are ringing as Nikki Benjamin wraps up the HERE COME THE BRIDES series with the heartwarming story of a hometown hero who convinces his childhood sweetheart to become his *Expectant Bride-To-Be.*

I hope all of these breathtaking romances warm your hearts and add joy to your holiday season.

Best,
Karen Taylor Richman
Senior Editor

Lara's Lover

PENNY RICHARDS

SPECIAL EDITION™

Published by Silhouette Books

America's Publisher of Contemporary Romance

This book is for Donovan Blaze Gorena,
handsome tough guy and potential heartbreaker.

Love ya, Blaze.

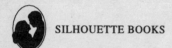 SILHOUETTE BOOKS

ISBN 0-373-24366-9

LARA'S LOVER

Copyright © 2000 by Penny Richards

This edition published by arrangement with Harlequin Books S.A.

® and TM are trademarks of Harlequin Books S.A., used under license.
Trademarks indicated with ® are registered in the United States Patent
and Trademark Office, the Canadian Trade Marks Office and in other
countries.

Visit Silhouette at www.eHarlequin.com

Printed in U.S.A.

Books by Penny Richards

PENNY RICHARDS

has also written under the pseudonym Bay Matthews and has been writing for Silhouette for sixteen years. She's been a cosmetologist, and award-winning artist and worked briefly as an interior decorator. She also served a brief stint as a short-order cook in her daughter-in-law's café. Claiming *everything* interests her, she collects dolls, books and antiques, and loves movies, reading, cooking, catalogs, redoing old houses, learning how to do anything new, Jeff Bridges, music by Yanni, poetry by Rod McKuen, yard sales and flea markets (she loves finding a bargain), gardening (she's a master gardener) and baseball. She has three children and nine grandchildren and lives in Arkansas with her husband of thirty-six years in a soon-to-be-one-hundred-year-old Queen Anne house listed on the National Register of Historic Places. She supports and works with her local garden club, arts league, literacy council and Friends of the Library. Always behind, she dreams of simplifying her life. Unfortunately, another deadline looms and there is paper to be hung and baseboards to refinish....

MISSOURI

TENNESSEE

● Fayetteville

Lewiston ●

● Fort Smith

Mississippi River

OKLAHOMA

Little Rock

★

ARKANSAS

MISSISSIPPI

N

TEXAS

LOUISIANA

All underlined places are fictitious

Chapter One

Donovan Delaney stripped the short-sleeved chambray shirt he'd just put on from his new jeans and tossed it to the bed where it joined a plaid golf shirt. Too plain, he thought. And it was starting to fade. He went to the closet and braced his arms on the doorjamb, examining the contents with a critical eye. The Hawaiian print shirt his niece, Cassidy, had given him for his birthday? No. It didn't convey the right image. neither did the maroon-and-taupe-striped button-down collar. Maybe the—

What the heck are you doing, Delaney? You're going to the high school to look things over and prepare a bid for some landscaping. You aren't going courting, and you aren't trying to impress anyone. It's summertime. Lara probably won't even be there.

"Right," he said aloud. He'd blown the whole thing out of proportion. But ever since he'd given up his position at a thriving landscape business in Baton Rouge and moved back to Lewiston, Arkansas, lots of things had happened, including his running into Lara Hardisty and realizing for sure that the nagging feeling that he'd never gotten over her was justified.

Even after seventeen years—during which she'd married, borne a child and gotten divorced—Lara still had the power to excite him. And infuriate him. And make him feel less than he'd come to know he was. No, never that. Any inferiority he might feel came from inside himself, not from Lara. Not once during the five years of his youth when he'd maintained the Graysons' lawns and flower beds had Lara ever made him feel second-rate.

In fact, the opposite was true. She had always made him feel he was more than the son of the town drunk. More than a punching bag for his father's frustrations, something he'd confided to her after a particularly bad session with Hutch.

Forget the past. Easier said than done, especially when it kept intruding on the future. Just two weeks before, Donovan and his sister, Sophie, had been discussing Sophie's past relationship with Reed Hardisty—who happened to be Lara's ex-husband—and Sophie's sixteen-year-old daughter had overheard. Cassidy had been more than a little upset to learn that Jake Carlisle, the man she'd grown up thinking was her father, wasn't, and she'd run away from her mother and the truth.

Thankfully, after a few tense hours, Lara and Reed's daughter, Belle, had confessed to knowing where Cassidy was, and she and the adults involved had talked things through. Sophie had also confessed to Reed that she—not Donovan—had been the one to shoot their father, after she'd taken physical abuse from him for refusing to abort Reed's baby.

Against Donovan's wishes, she'd called the sheriff and confessed, saying she was telling him so Donovan could start his life over with a clean slate. Thankfully, Sheriff Lawrence had listened and then told them it was all in the past as far as he was concerned. No matter who had pulled the trigger, Donovan had paid the price by spending several years in prison. Sophie wasn't a killer, and it was all water under the bridge. They should forget the past and go on about their lives.

Which was what Sophie and Reed had been trying to do ever since. Realizing that they still cared about each other, they had decided not to rush into marriage. They were giving themselves a few months, trying to get to know each other again, while Reed forged a relationship with his newly discovered daughter. Neither Sophie nor Reed wanted to make another mistake.

Donovan didn't want to make any more mistakes, either. He'd acted rashly when he'd taken the blame for his sister's crime, and he would do it again if necessary, but he'd spent too many years putting his life back together to wreck it by pursuing a woman who clearly still held a grudge for the things that had happened between them seventeen years before. He'd come back to town to put in a nursery and landscape business, and he had no intention of giving the rumormongers fodder for the small-town gossip mill. He wouldn't go looking for Lara; he'd just see what developed.

So stop actin' like some prissy woman and worryin' about what you're going to look like just in case you do run into her.

"Right," Donovan said again, his expression and

his voice grim. He slammed the closet door shut and reached into the drawer for one of the many gray pocket T-shirts he'd had printed with his company logo. Then, just to prove something to himself, he peeled the new jeans off and replaced them with a pair of faded, well-worn denims with a small hole in the thigh, the result of a minor skirmish with a maverick nail. In a purely masculine gesture, he smoothed the placket flat, scooped his battered sneakers from the floor and headed for the kitchen he'd remodeled recently.

The room was empty without Sophie and Cass, who'd gone back to Baton Rouge, but Sophie had claimed she had a lot to do before she and Cassidy could move to Lewiston and start over, hopefully before school started in August. Donovan sighed. Knowing the situation didn't make him any less lonely.

He opened the refrigerator and grabbed the gallon of chocolate milk he'd bought the day before, reaching for a glass with his other hand. He found a honey bun in the pantry and ripped open the package with his teeth. With Sophie's dire warnings about his abominable eating habits echoing in his head, he took a healthy bite and washed it down with the milk. *Ah. Breakfast of champions.*

It wasn't as if he was trying to set an example of good eating habits for anyone, he thought, polishing off the sweet in a matter of minutes. There was no one but himself. Realizing that he was about to fall into a bout of self-pity, he finished the milk, rinsed the glass and put it in the dishwasher. Then he headed for his truck, his measuring tape, drawing pad and a couple of sharp pencils in hand.

* * *

There were several cars in the parking lot when Donovan arrived. It didn't take him long to realize summer school was in session, which meant there was at least a fifty-fifty chance Lara was on the premises. He wasn't sure whether that pleased or annoyed him. Reminding himself that he was there to do a job and telling himself his whole future might hang on his professionalism, he set to work.

The high school was relatively new, no more than five years old. The first thing he did was make a cursory inspection of the grounds, looking at what was planted and how it was faring. Lara was soon forgotten. It was easy to see that the architects had spared no expense when it came to design and building, or the landscaping for that matter. But as usual, when care was negligible, a lot of plants hadn't survived. He noted places where shrubs had died, the soil was eroding and the grass had been tromped on by careless feet. The demise of various perennials in the flower beds along the front of the building gave a spotty, tired and neglected air to an otherwise agreeable facade.

Donovan went to his truck and got his pad and a pencil. It wouldn't be necessary to make a drawing. What had been done was fine. All he had to do was make a notation of how many and what kinds of plants and shrubs he'd need to bring the place back up to snuff.

Lara left the gymnasium, frowning. She'd been summoned by a young substitute teacher to settle an argument between a girl and her recently discarded boyfriend. The situation troubled her. Lexie Jamerson was a nice girl, a good student. Darren Poteet was from a middle-class family, also good people, but Darren had begun to show signs of rebellion ever since his dad walked out on the family, leaving his mother to deal single-handedly with four children.

Darren hadn't taken the news that Lexie wanted to move on very well, no doubt considering it another abandonment. He continued to harass her about their getting back together. It was a sad, yet volatile, situation that showed no signs of getting better. Darren had actually pushed Lexie before Lara and Mr. Jacobs, the hefty maintenance man arrived. She'd told Darren that she wanted him to make an appointment with the school counselor as soon as possible and that she would talk to his mother. Other than that, there was nothing Lara could do.

She picked up her pace, eager to get back to her office. It would soon be time to call it a day. She saw Donovan's truck before she saw him. Her heart leaped, went into free fall and then began to beat in double time, a reaction that did not please her in the least. Telling herself that whatever feelings she might have had for Donovan Delaney had died when he cut her out of his life with all the skill of a top surgeon did nothing toward calming her fluttering pulse.

She squared her shoulders and, walking even faster, crossed the grassy area that led to the door of the building where her office was situated. Head high, she rounded the building. In her peripheral vision she saw something rise from the ground in a fluidlike motion. Before she could stop, she'd run smack-dab into something big and warm and rock hard. Something hit her chin with enough force to bring tears to her eyes and cause her teeth to snap together. Closing her eyes against the pain, she staggered back a step, thankful she hadn't bitten her tongue. Her upper arms were taken in a firm grip.

"Are you okay?"

The deep, sexy, Sam Elliott-like voice was one that had haunted her dreams for more years than she cared to admit. Her knees buckled, and she clutched at his arms to keep from falling. She'd heard that voice whispering endearments, singing pop ballads and hard rock, heard it growling pleasure in her ear. She was grateful for the pain, which gave legitimacy to the tears filling her eyes. She tried to summon her anger, but it was hard with him touching her, and her mind flooded with bits and pieces of a hundred delicious memories.

"Lara?"

She swallowed, still unable to speak, and nodded. "I'm okay," she managed to get out at the same time she forced her eyelids upward. She clamped her teeth down on her quivering lower lip and stared up at him, hoping she wouldn't start bawling and make a complete fool of herself. He was frowning, his dark eyebrows drawn into a single straight line above worried, cobalt-blue eyes. She'd forgotten how sexy his mouth was. She'd also forgotten how absurdly long his eyelashes were—the only thing about Donovan Delaney that wasn't uncompromisingly male.

"Are you sure?"

"Sure?" she repeated, having no idea what he was talking about.

"Are you sure you're okay?"

She nodded again.

"If your chin hurts as badly as the top of my head, you're lying through your teeth—if you still have teeth," he added with a half smile. He lifted her chin with his index finger.

Lara steeled herself against his touch and smiled back, albeit weakly.

"Yeah, you still have teeth. You may have a bruise tomorrow," he added. "Where were you going in such an all-fired hurry?"

"Back to my office. What are you doing here?" She knew exactly why he was there, but she wanted to steer the conversation away from herself.

"Isabelle asked me to come and take a look at the grounds and see what it would take to get them back in top-notch shape."

"That's right." She stepped back to put some distance between them. "I'd better let you get to work, then."

"I'm almost finished. I was taking some soil samples."

"Oh. Well, good luck."

"How's Belle?" he asked.

She blinked. Where had that come from? "Belle?"

"Belle. Your daughter."

He was laughing at her, she thought, noting the mockery dancing in his eyes. She managed a fair bit of indignation. "I know who Belle is. It just surprised me that you asked about her, that's all."

"Why should that surprise you? Just because I don't have any kids doesn't mean I don't like them."

"I realize that," she said a bit tartly. "She's fine."

"How is she taking to the idea of having Sophie for a stepmom?"

"I think she's adjusting to the idea very well, and she's crazy about Cassidy."

"And how about you?"

"Me?" she asked, caught off guard again.

Donovan shifted his weight to one leg and crossed

his arms over his broad chest. "Yeah, you. How are you taking it?"

She shrugged. "I still care about Reed, and I want him to be happy. If Sophie makes him happy, I'm all for the marriage."

The mockery vanished, replaced by another frown. "So you have regrets about your failed marriage?"

From somewhere inside a building, a bell rang, signaling the end of class. The jangling sound jolted her to her senses. Why was he asking her all these questions? She didn't want to talk about her marriage to Reed. Didn't want to think about the past and her failures. Any of them.

"Not that it's any of your business, Mr. Delaney, but of course I have regrets. I believe all failures produce some degree of regret, don't you?"

"What I regret is that you used to call me Donovan," he said. "And if you still care for him, why did you give him a divorce?"

"The deterioration of my marriage is none of your concern," she told him, resorting to the cool formality she used with recalcitrant students. Even as she felt her lips curve in a chilly smile, she realized she sounded like her great-aunt. "Oh, and I still think of you as Donovan in my mind when I happen to think about the past. And when I think about the way you dumped me, I call you lots of things, none of them as polite as Donovan or Mr. Delaney."

To her surprise he laughed. Laughed! She brushed past him. "Goodbye, Mr. Delaney."

He took her upper arm in a firm but gentle grip. "Whoa!"

Lara had no choice but to stop. She turned to face him. His amused gaze seemed drawn to her breasts, which were rising and falling beneath the simple, round-necked shell she wore. He lifted his gaze to her face. She stood stock-still, like a deer caught in the headlights of an oncoming car, mesmerized by the expression in his eyes, remembering…

"Hi, Ms. Hardisty," came a girlish chorus as a trio of young women passed by, clearly curious about what was going on between her and Donovan.

Lara looked pointedly at his hand on her arm, even as she forced herself to smile and say, "Good morning, ladies."

As they turned the corner, they cast one last look at Donovan, then rounded the building, smothering their giggles behind their hands.

"What's the hurry?" he asked, releasing her. "I might get the idea you don't like my company."

She squared her shoulders and looked at him through a narrowed gaze. She felt as gauche and immature as the girls who'd just passed, the same way she'd felt with Donovan before he'd begun to show any interest in her. "I don't."

"Oh, I think you do, and that's the problem."

"I don't have a problem," she said, knowing as she did so that it was a lie. "But this is America. Think what you will."

She turned and started down the sidewalk.

"I plan to," he said to her back. "Hey! Do you still wear that sexy underwear?"

She gasped at his audacity, the question bringing her to a stop. A wave of memory swept over her. The two of them lying on a quilt in the back of his beat-up pickup beneath an ebony velvet sky dusted with starlight. Donovan undoing her blouse, trailing his fingertip teasingly over he edge of the lacy bra and the crest of her breast… A moan of need—her moan—spilling from her lips into the silence of the night. Another of those memories that crept up annoyingly whenever she least expected it.

She wanted to scream out her frustration, wanted to tell him to leave her alone, wanted to ask him why he'd come back and disrupted her happy life. She refused to turn around and look at him.

"That's for me to know and you to find out."

As soon as the provocative answer left her lips, she wondered where it had come from. She felt like Jim Carrey in the movie, *Liar Liar*. Forced to be truthful no matter what she *meant* to say. She started down the sidewalk at a brisk pace.

"Is that a dare, Ms. Hardisty, ma'am?" he called out from behind her. Her footsteps faltered. "'Cause if it is, I never was one to turn down a dare."

The implications of that taunt sent a rush of fiery heat through Lara's body. She whirled to face him, taking what refuge she could in her anger. "Why are you doing this? Do you get some perverse kind of pleasure from tormenting me?"

"Is that what I'm doing?" he asked. "Tormenting you?"

"You know you are."

"Funny. I thought putting myself under your sharp tongue was self-torment."

Not bothering to look at the deeper meaning of his reply, she shook her head. "Then why do it?"

He shrugged. "I can't seem to help myself."

Something about the honesty in his eyes tugged at Lara's heart, but she'd fallen for his line before and ended up with a broken heart. She couldn't go through that again. She was no longer an insecure young woman looking for acceptance and approval wherever she could find it. She was older and hopefully wiser.

"Try harder," she said in her most schoolteacherly voice.

"I'll do my best."

The words were spoken with the utmost solemnity, but that glimmer of mischief was back in his blue eyes. Lara drew a sharp, unsteady breath, turned on her heel and walked away, cursing whatever it was that had brought him back into her comfortable, stable world. Wondering exactly what that something was and finally admitting to the truth she'd tried so hard not to face: she'd never really gotten over Donovan Delaney. Never put him and their past fully behind her.

The realization brought her to another halt, then sent her steps into fast forward, as if by putting as much distance as possible between herself and him she could outrun the truth. It didn't work. When she pushed through the door to the cool interior of the building she was as agitated as ever.

She paused in the doorway, closed her eyes and pressed her palms to her hot cheeks with a little groan of dismay. What was she going to do? How could she live a normal life with Donovan living right on her doorstep, so to speak? Ignoring him would be impossible in a town the size of Lewiston. Ignoring her feelings would be even harder. But ignore them she would. He'd hurt her once, stomped her pride in the dirt by rejecting her when she wanted nothing more than to offer him her love and support.

"Are you all right, Ms. Hardisty?"

Lara opened her eyes. Lucy McClarty, the school secretary, had poked her head out the glass divider that

separated the hall from the outer office, an expression
of concern on her dark face.

Lara forced a weak smile. "I'm fine, Lucy. I think
I just got a little hot or something."

"It's hotter'n Hades out there," Lucy agreed. "Go
on into your office and sit down. I'll bring you a cola."

"That sounds wonderful. Thanks."

A new thought hit her. Not only would it be personal ruin to get involved with Donovan Delaney, it
would be professional suicide. She'd worked hard to
get where she was, worked harder to see to it that
nothing spoiled her image of competence. She was a
woman with a job that, in places like Lewiston, was
considered a man's domain. She'd been careful not to
get involved with the wrong kind of man, not to do
anything that might put a blot on her immaculate record. She didn't intend to let Donovan or any leftover
feelings she might have for him change that. Her job
meant too much to her.

*Aren't you getting ahead of yourself, Lara? Dono-
van didn't say a word about wanting to get involved
with you.* He hadn't, not in so many words. But he
wanted to. She'd known him a long time and recognized that look in his eyes for what it was. Determination. She wasn't sure what had brought him back,
but since he was here, he might as well kill two birds
with one stone. He was a man with a mission. And
she was his objective.

Donovan watched her go, knowing he'd revealed
more of his feelings than he'd intended. Far more than
was smart. But it was done, she was gone, and there
was no taking it back. There was nothing to do but
enjoy the play of fabric stretched across her hips and

admire the way the chunky heels of her shoes en-
hanced the calves of her legs. *Did* she still wear that
sexy underwear? He vowed to find out—one way or
the other.

Lucy brought the cola and Lara sipped at it while
she relived the unsettling encounter with Donovan.
Unsettling? Ha! Disastrous might be a better description. She'd been a wreck ever since he'd come back
to Lewiston four weeks earlier—not to mention short-
tempered and cranky. Belle was constantly asking her
if she had PMS, which only made things worse. Nor
did it help that her ex-husband was deliriously happy
at being reunited with his youthful love. He kept telling her that her time would come, but Lara had been
forced to take a pragmatic approach to life. She didn't
believe in fairy tales.

Lara and her brother, Wes, had been left without a
mother when Victoria Grayson was killed in a car
crash when they were eight and eleven. From that
point on, they were brought up by a series of house-
keepers. Their father, Phil Grayson, along with Leo
Duncan, Lara's great-aunt Isabelle's husband, owned
the local bank and had been far too busy with his various business schemes and his own grief to help his
children deal with theirs.

At best, Phil was an absentee father. At worst, he'd
neglected them—not that they were ever mistreated or
lacked the necessities. In fact, the opposite had been
true. Both she and Wes had had the best money could
buy. Unfortunately, money has never been a satisfactory substitute for love. Lara, who adored her older
brother, had wanted to spend more time with him. But
Weston, who'd inherited their mother's artistic ability

and temperament, had been perfectly content to be alone with his charcoal and oils, surrounded by the scent of turpentine and drying paint. When he'd wanted company, he sought out Reed, and the two of them went off and did whatever guys did to entertain themselves. Lara was left alone and lonely, searching for a purpose.

Naturally a kind and caring person, she'd become the caregiver, making sure her father's shirts were dropped off at the laundry, making certain Wes's clothes were laid out for school the next day. Neither noticed, or if they did, they never commented on it.

When Lara was in the eighth grade, the family moved to a brand-new house, leaving behind the big two-story where she'd grown up. Lara hated the new house, and so did Wes, though he never said anything. She told her father she and Wes didn't need baby-sitters anymore and that she wanted to take over the running of the house, since it wasn't nearly as big as the old one. Knowing she was capable, Phil agreed.

The glorified baby-sitters were let go. Lara begged her great-aunt Isabelle to "loan" her Ruby Delaney one day a week. Lara was already becoming quite a cook, and all she needed was someone to help with the hardest tasks. When it came time to hire someone to take care of the yard, it seemed natural for Ruby's son, who did Isabelle's yard work, to take on the job.

Donovan was seventeen when he came to work for the Graysons. He reminded Lara of the pictures of the statues in her mother's books—all smooth muscle and bronze skin. Though she didn't see him weekly once the mowing season was over, he was around throughout the year, picking up limbs and raking leaves in the fall, readying the flower beds in winter, planting in the spring and mowing during the summer.

Donovan didn't pay much attention to her that first year. Unlike Justine Sutton, who was a year behind her in school, Lara wasn't that well endowed. She was taller than most of her peers, leggy and slender, more classically beautiful than pretty, blessed with the kind of bone structure that comes into its own with the accumulation of years.

During the first couple of years, Donovan was more like her big brother than Wes. He listened when Wes wouldn't. He teased, tugged her ponytail and listened to her girlish chatter. By the time she was a sophomore, she was totally and completely smitten, and she knew by the way he looked at her that he liked her, too. They opened up even more to each other and fought their mutual attraction throughout her junior year, while Lara headed up the debate team and Donovan, who worked more than forty hours a week, struggled through basic classes at the nearby community college.

He finally kissed her during Christmas break of her senior year, and they started dating secretly that winter. She was eighteen and loved him with all her heart. They dated on the sly for several months, and foolishly she'd given him both her heart and her body. At the time it seemed like the natural and right thing to do, like drawing a next, much-needed breath. She would have dated him openly, but he would have none of it. He didn't want her classmates looking down on her, didn't want people laughing at her because she was Donovan Delaney's girl. When he finally proposed, he wanted to bring something to the marriage besides his dad's bad name.

So they'd loved each other in secret, dreaming dreams and making plans while Donovan saved his hard-earned money and made arrangements to apply for a scholarship and some grant money to finish out his schooling. She would get her education degree and they would get married. It was a good plan. A workable plan. They were in no hurry. They had each other and all the time in the world. Or so they thought.

Lara knew about Hutch Delaney's abuse and that Donovan often took the brunt of his father's anger when he took up the cause for his mother and sister. She tended his cuts and scrapes, kissed his bruises and prayed Hutch Delaney would die. Unfortunately, she hadn't been specific enough in her prayers. She hadn't expected Donovan to shoot his father to protect himself and Sophie. Hadn't expected him to be arrested, carted off to jail and sent to prison, mere days before she found out she was pregnant. She certainly never imagined that he would refuse to see her, read her letters or take her calls once he'd been placed in the county jail. But he had, and his abandonment had very nearly destroyed her.

Of course, the jailer had informed her father of her calls and visits, and there had been hell to pay. When Lara, confused and frightened, realized she couldn't hide her pregnancy, she'd had no choice but to confess her predicament to her dad, who confided to his good friend, Rowland Hardisty, and asked Rowland to suggest a good doctor for an abortion. Instead, Rowland suggested that Reed and Lara marry. Wasn't that his and Phil's lifelong dream?

Neither Reed nor Lara had enough backbone to stand up to their fathers, but that didn't matter. They were both hurting and confused, and, with the shortsightedness of youth, neither of them could see what might happen to them and their marriage a few years down the road. She liked Reed, and he liked her, but there was no spark there, and probably never would be. On some level they both realized that, but at that moment neither of them cared.

Angry at Donovan and fearful of being whispered about if news of her pregnancy got out, Lara agreed, with the stipulation that her father not tell a soul who her baby's father was. He agreed. Surprisingly, Reed had accepted that, too. He'd never asked her whose baby she was carrying. It was only later, when she found out about his feelings for Sophie, that Lara realized the true reason behind his acceptance of the Grayson-Hardisty plan. Wes, who was behaving a little strangely himself, told them they were both crazy, but in the end, he accepted the marriage between his best friend and his sister.

In a nutshell, Reed was searching for a way to get out from under his father's thumb and to forget Sophie, who by that time had left town. Lara wanted to salvage her reputation and give her baby a name. So they married, figuring that when news about the baby got out, people would think it was Reed's. As her father pointed out, it was fortuitous that she had dated Reed briefly and publicly while she was seeing Donovan in secret.

So they married, their respective fathers maintaining it was a fine, workable solution to everyone's problems. But fate, as Lara and Reed had both already learned, plays havoc with lives and plans and schemes, and it played another cruel joke. Just three weeks after she married Reed, she lost Donovan's baby, and all the subterfuge was for nothing.

For all that they'd mouthed the right platitudes at the time, Lara was smart enough to realize that both her father and Rowland were thrilled that she'd lost the baby. She was desolate, and if it hadn't been for Reed, she wasn't sure what she'd have done. Seeing her devastation, he consoled her as best he could. He was her only friend, and the loss of the baby drew them closer. Rowland and Phil worried that they might separate with no reason to stay together and were pleased when they showed no desire to split up.

Eventually, Lara and Reed healed enough to realize that they were young and healthy with all the desires and needs of young, healthy people. Since they were both content in the arrangement and neither was inclined to look elsewhere, it became a marriage in every sense of the word.

Days drifted into weeks and months and years. They were compatible and seldom argued. But after a few years they began to see more clearly what they'd known from the beginning. They loved each other, but they weren't in love. Hoping a baby might bring them closer, Lara got pregnant. Belle was conceived on the night they were both a little tipsy from too much champagne, both thinking of the past. The night Reed called Lara by Sophie's name as they both reached their release.

Lara knew who he meant, and she gave serious consideration to giving him a divorce. By the time she'd worked up enough courage to face not only him but their respective fathers, she'd discovered she was pregnant, and she knew she owed it to herself and to Reed to stick out the marriage for the baby's sake.

Belle, who embodied the best of Lara and Reed, had come into the world kicking and screaming. Her arriv-

al livened up their lives, but not in the way they'd
hoped. When she was six years old, after eleven mundane years of marriage, they agreed to call it quits. As
every other aspect of their relationship, the break was
clean, civil and passionless, and Lara was much happier not living a lie.

They both dated, Lara less often than Reed, who
was considered the catch of the town. She didn't think
she'd ever marry again since she'd given her heart so
completely to Donovan. Feeling the need to make
some sort of mark of her own, she applied for the
position of principal and landed it by the skin of her
teeth. The good-old-boy mentality was still very much
in place in Lewiston, and there were those who didn't
think she deserved the position, who didn't think she
could handle it, and those who were waiting for her to
make the slightest mistake, so they could claim, "I
told you so."

Lara was good at her job and knew it. She was compassionate without being a pushover. Friendly but firm.
Unlike her predecessor, she genuinely liked teenage
kids. So far, she'd been lucky. There had been no major problems, no scandals, nothing a little common
sense, intelligence and diplomacy hadn't fixed.

But that was before Donovan Delaney had come to
town and shaken her world, her complacency and her
heart. It made her furious that he could still rouse any
emotion in her, even though that emotion was anger.
Of course, like any intelligent woman, she'd known
from the moment she'd set eyes on him, the day he'd
come to pick up Cassidy, that the anger was just a
cover-up for something she wasn't ready to admit to
feeling. Something she was afraid she would never be
ready to admit to feeling.

Chapter Two

Donovan was still calling himself a fool on Wednesday, two days later. Since his encounter with Lara, he'd hardly slept, spending the long hours of the night reliving the precious moments of their past relationship and poring over wholesale catalogues and price guides, trying to decide what plants to buy in an effort to block the memories of her from his mind.

During the day he and Jett Robbins, a nineteen-year-old local boy who'd been helping him with the construction of the greenhouses, worked beneath the broiling sun, stretching the heavy clear plastic skin over the skeletal forms and laying the PVC pipe that would be used for watering. Donovan's only breaks came when someone called, asking a question or wanting him to come and take a look at their yard to see what could be done to make things more inviting.

To his surprise the fliers that he, Sophie and Cassidy

had passed out at the Woodcutters' Festival had generated a considerable amount of business. It helped that there was a growing interest in gardening and expanding living space by adding outdoor living areas. With any luck the trend would continue, at least for the next few years.

He was sitting at the kitchen table, washing down powdered-sugar doughnuts with chocolate milk and bemoaning the fact that the house was so empty, when the phone rang.

"Hey!" came a feminine voice when he answered.

"Hey, yourself!" he said to his sister. "What are you doing up so early?"

"Trying to get everything done before Cassidy and I head back that direction. You don't mind putting us up, do you?"

"That's a stupid question," Donovan said. "I was just sitting here feeling sorry for myself because it's so lonely. When are you coming?"

"Poor baby. We're flying out on Friday morning. Can you pick us up at the Little Rock Airport at eleven-twenty? Reed has to be in court."

"Sure. I'll give Jett the morning off. Of course, I'm sure he'll want to be here in the afternoon, since Cass is coming. I think he's really smitten with her."

"You aren't easing my mind any, big brother."

Jett was three years older than Cassidy. He had that dangerous combination of good looks, cocky self-assurance and disregard for authority that made the mothers of teenage daughters want to go to the nearest store to look for a chastity belt. According to Reed, Jett had been in a few scrapes, but nothing serious. His dad was dead, and he just needed a firmer hand than his single mom could give him.

Donovan laughed. "He's really a pretty good kid."

"Would you want him dating your daughter?"

"I wouldn't be opposed to it, if I thought she knew the score, which Cassidy does."

"She does know that," Sophie said, referring to Cassidy learning the painful truth about Sophie and Reed's youthful relationship.

They'd all learned plenty, Donovan thought. Not only had Reed found out Cassidy was his daughter—something he'd had no idea of—both he and Sophie had learned that their fathers had lied to them, possibly robbing them of seventeen years together. According to Sophie, Reed's resentment went so deep he was still barely speaking to his father. Cassidy had learned that Reed, not the deceased Jake Carlisle, was her father and that despite her mother's warnings about the dangers of becoming sexually active, she'd been just that at Cassidy's age.

"You really think it's okay for her to see him?"

"They're kids, Sis. They're breathing and they have normal sex drives. She's as safe with him as she'd be with any boy his age. She's the one who controls how far things will go."

Sophie's sigh filtered through the phone lines. "You're right, as usual. Maybe you should be the counselor."

Donovan heard the beep that told him he had another call coming in. "I've got another call. Hold on."

"No. I have to go. Just pick us up Friday."

"Eleven-twenty. Got it. Tell Cass I'll buy her Chinese for lunch."

Sophie laughed. "I will. See you."

Donovan said goodbye and took the other call.

"Donovan? Isabelle Duncan."

"Good morning, Miss Isabelle," Donovan said, a genuine smile curving his lips. "You're up and at 'em bright and early this morning."

Like her voice, Isabelle's laugh sounded rusty, as if she seldom used it—a Lauren Bacall voice with an extra roughness from a fifty-year, two-pack-a-day cigarette habit.

"When you get to be my age, you're lucky to sleep beyond four in the morning. And then you embarrass yourself by drifting off into those little catnaps every time you sit down."

This time it was Donovan's turn to laugh. "What can I do for you, Miss Isabelle?"

"I was wondering if you'd been to the school yet."

"Yes, ma'am. I went a couple of days ago and took an inventory of what I'd need to get things back ship-shape. I've been working up a proposal between things around here."

"No hurry," Isabelle said. "As long as it's done before school starts."

"Then we have plenty of time."

"So what do you think about the upcoming nuptials?"

Donovan was caught off guard. To his knowledge Isabelle wasn't a gossip. But then, this wasn't gossip. She was just asking his opinion about the future of two people they were both close to.

"I think if they still care for each other, the wedding is long overdue. And I don't think it ever hurts for the truth to be known, no matter how painful it may be."

"Hmm," Isabelle said. "I like your sister—what I've seen of her, and I believe she'll be good for Reed. He and my niece tried their best to make their marriage work, but there was just no spark there, and they both finally lost heart.''

"It happens," Donovan said. He was hardly the one to be discussing Lara's marital failure, since he was thrilled that she was a free woman.

"I worry about Lara, though," Isabelle said, her tone thoughtful. "She's bright, pretty and has a lot to offer, but she hardly dates."

News that didn't upset Donovan at all.

"She takes her job very seriously, and I worry that she's so concerned about offending the people in this town that she'll turn into a dried-up old maid."

"I doubt that will happen," Donovan said. Not if he had anything to say about it. "She's young. There's plenty of time for her to find someone."

Isabelle snorted. "In Lewiston? Not unless someone comes along who will sweep her off her feet the way my Leo did me." She gave another hoarse chuckle. "I fought him and my family all the way to the altar. No one thought he was good enough for me. His father was just the local plumber, you know, but he was smart and did well at the bank. We had more than fifty wonderful years together." She sighed. "Money can't buy happiness, Donovan. Remember that. It's people who make you happy."

"I've already figured that out, Miss Isabelle."

"Then you're well ahead of the game." She laughed again. "Good grief! I'm getting absolutely maudlin in my old age. I didn't call to lecture you or to discuss my great-niece's love life. I called to ask you to come take a look at my gardens whenever it's convenient for you. You won't believe how wonderful your waterfall looks. And I also wanted to ask you if you'd take Lara's Belle under your wing."

"Belle?" he said. "What do you mean?"

"The child has a great interest in plants. She must get it from me," she added. "She likes tinkering around in the garden, and she's full of questions."

"She couldn't have a better teacher than you," Donovan said. "I can attest to that."

"It's kind of you to say so, but I'm sure you've far surpassed my meager horticultural knowledge. The problem is that I don't have the stamina I did even twenty years ago. The heat gets to me, and I can't get up and down as easily as I once did. I know you're busy, but if you had the inclination to let Belle follow along after you, I'd be eternally grateful. She's a fast learner and a hard worker."

Donovan wasn't sure how to answer. Being Cassidy's uncle represented his only experience with kids. He wasn't sure he could relate to a twelve-year-old child—especially a girl. On the other hand, Isabelle Duncan had gone out of her way to help him. He would never have been able to come back and follow his dream without her support and influence, and he felt obligated to do whatever he could to accommodate her—within reason.

There was also the fact that they were talking about Lara's daughter, and it might be smart of him to try to win her over. Letting Belle work with him also meant there was the off chance that Lara would be driving Belle back and forth.

"Sure," he heard himself saying. "I'd be glad to teach her what I can, if she's willing to listen and learn. When would she like to start?"

"I'll need to check with Lara. Belle has a fairly full summer schedule, so it may be that she can only come an hour or two here and there."

"That's fine," Donovan said, relieved that he wouldn't have her eight hours a day, five days a week. "I'm doing some planting at the Echolses' place tomorrow, if she can meet me there."

"Excellent. I don't think you'll be sorry, Donovan. I'm sure she'll be an apt pupil, and she'll be thrilled that you've agreed to teach her. Both Reed and Lara are quite intelligent, as I'm sure you know, and, as I said, Belle has a genuine interest in the whole growing process."

"It should work out well, then," Donovan said.

"I think so," Isabelle said, her husky voice coming close to a purr. "I'll give Lara a call and tell her about tomorrow. Belle can call and let you know if she can make it."

"Great."

"Yes," Isabelle said. "It is."

"It's out of the question," Lara said to her great-aunt, when Isabelle stopped by on her way to the beauty shop.

Isabelle's pale-blue eyes, which looked twice their normal size behind the thick, round-lens glasses she wore, blinked twice, reminding Lara of an owl.

"And why is that, dear?" Isabelle asked, her thinly plucked eyebrows drawn into a frown. "If it's his reputation you're worried about—"

"It has nothing to do with his reputation or the fact that he did time in prison," Lara interrupted. "I know Donovan would never...hurt Belle."

"Then I fail to see what you can possibly object to," Isabelle said in a soft voice. "The child is as smart as a whip. She's very interested in horticulture, and it seems to me it would be a chance to further her knowledge. Donovan has assured me he doesn't mind.''

"You've already talked to him?'' Lara asked, pausing and tucking a strand of hair behind her ear.

"Well, of course I have, dear. I didn't think it was fair to get Belle's hopes up only to have them dashed if Donovan didn't have the time to spare. But he's assured me that he doesn't mind taking her along with him when he's working around town. It isn't as if it will be every day.''

Belle had always loved the outdoors, and it was true that she showed an unusual interest in plants, which Lara attributed to her having spent so much time with Isabelle. Belle's interest had deepened when Isabelle gave her a book about the language of flowers and how the Victorians used tussie-mussies not only to hide body odor but to send messages to their peers. A lover of puzzles and games, the idea of trying to figure out exactly what a bouquet really meant had intrigued Belle, who now owned several books on the subject and liked to make posies herself for her teachers and friends.

There was no doubt that her spending time with Donovan would be beneficial. The problem was that Lara knew she would have to transport her daughter to and from the places Donovan was working, at least part of the time, and she wasn't sure she wanted to take a chance on seeing him every few days.

"Well?'' Isabelle asked.

"I'll tell Belle and let her decide. I won't always be available to take her, but I suppose she can ride her bike most places in town.''

"Probably so.'' Isabelle pushed herself to her feet.

"I'm sure Donovan won't mind picking her up if necessary."

"Oh, I hope not!"

"Lara, my dear," Isabelle said. "What is your problem?" She reached up and took Lara's chin, squeezing with fingers tipped with long, red-lacquered nails. Her faded blue eyes held concern and what looked like understanding. "Whatever Donovan Delaney did happened a long time ago, Lara. He's paid, and dearly. God knows, *everyone* has paid. People do what they do for reasons we can only guess at, my dear. Sometimes we don't understand, especially when those decisions affect us directly or bring us pain."

Though nothing had been said about Donovan turning his back on her when he was incarcerated, Lara couldn't help feeling her aunt was talking about just that. But how could she be, when no one had known she and Donovan were seeing each other?

"Aunt Isabelle," she said, choosing her words carefully. "What are you talking about?"

Isabelle blinked again and released her hold on Lara's chin with a tender pat, sort of like an afterthought. "Why, Donovan's decision to stand up for himself and his sister, of course. I'm sure he didn't think about the repercussions when he...did what he did. He just acted. And thank God he did."

"Aunt Isabelle!" Lara cried in astonishment. Her aunt abhorred violence of any kind and was so tenderhearted she wouldn't even kill spiders, trapping them and releasing them outside instead.

"Hutch Delaney was a weak man who treated his family abominably when he was in the bottle, which was 99 percent of the time." Isabelle gave a delicate shudder. "I saw what he did to Ruby on more than one occasion, and I heard about how he treated his children—though I had to pry it out of her.''

Her eyes filled with tears. Ruby Delaney had kept house for her for more than thirty years before her death, during which time the two women had grown to like and respect each other, though they'd never stepped beyond the bounds of employer and employee in public. ''I give Ruby a lot of credit for managing to bring up two decent, productive citizens in spite of the wretch she was married to.''

''I don't understand why you're telling me this,'' Lara said, fearing that her aunt, whose mind had always been so sharp, was beginning to slip.

Isabelle's eyes widened with candor, and with the lift of one shoulder, she sank back into her chair. ''You seem uneasy about Belle spending time with Donovan. I'm just trying to point out that a mistake or a bad decision can be punishment enough in itself. Once they're made, we have to live with them, move on. Fretting over them only makes us bitter and hard.'' She smiled. ''Take you, for example. I'm sure you had your reasons for marrying Reed, and he had his for marrying you, even though you didn't love each other.''

Lara gasped.

''Oh, don't act so shocked,'' Isabelle said with a dismissive wave of her hand. ''A blind man could see the two of you had absolutely no interest in that marriage or each other. As a matter of fact, neither of you had much interest in anything back then, as I recall. At first I thought you might be pregnant, but when time rocked on and there was no baby, I had to discount that theory.''

Lara's mind raced. Why was her aunt bringing all

this up now, when they'd never discussed her marriage—not even when it was falling apart? Maybe, Lara thought, the recent happenings with Reed and Sophie had brought it all back. And Isabelle was getting old.

Isabelle smiled. "But whatever the reasons, you and Reed lived with your mistake and tried to make the best of it. I've admired the two of you for holding on as long as you did. I admire you more for staying friends for Belle's sake."

"It has nothing to do with Belle. I like Reed."

Isabelle nodded. "He's a good man, in spite of having Rowland Hardisty for a father. Though she's about as visible as a speck on the wallpaper in Rowland's life, Celeste Hardisty did a good job of counteracting his influence in their son. And you're a good girl, Lara Elizabeth. You deserve some real happiness."

"Thank you, Aunt Isabelle."

Isabelle laughed. "I guess we know why Reed married you now, but your reasons for marrying him are still a mystery."

The idea that Isabelle was still fascinated with Lara's motivation brought a spurt of panic. She managed a small smile. "Oh. And why do you think Reed married me?"

"To try to forget Sophia, of course. Obviously, she either didn't tell him about her pregnancy before she left town, or she didn't know. Either way, I think it's safe to assume that Reed still felt something for her, so he either married you to try to get back at her in case she did come back to town, or he did it to try to forget her."

Lara, who, only moments before was concerned

about her aunt's faculties, was now amazed at the complexity of Isabelle's thought processes.

"At any rate, mistake or not, the two of you got Belle out of the deal, so it was worth it in my book, don't you agree?"

Lara nodded and then sat quietly for a moment, staring at her aunt with a considering expression and wondering what was going on.

Isabelle laughed her rusty laugh. "I'm getting old and garrulous, aren't I?" she asked, but her eyes looked shrewd, sharp. "I simply wanted to say that whatever Donovan did in the past is over and done with, just like your marriage to Reed. You and Reed paid. Donovan paid. Don't make him keep paying."

Once again, Lara couldn't shake the feeling that her aunt knew more about Lara's past relationship with Donovan than she was admitting to. She thought about the hurt and bitterness she still felt toward Donovan for the way he'd cut her out of his life. "Is that what I'm doing?" she asked, not trying to camouflage her own meaning.

Isabelle didn't bat an eye. Their gazes locked in complete understanding, and in that one instant Lara knew that somehow, without a doubt, they were both talking about the same thing: her feelings about Donovan.

"Aren't you?" Isabelle asked in a gentle voice.

Before Lara could rally for a reply, the back door slammed, and the moment passed. The next thing Lara knew, Isabelle was once again pushing herself to her tiny feet, which were encased in strappy, open-toed shoes straight from the forties.

"If Belle ever needs a ride to meet Donovan, just call. I'll have Rodney pick her up and deliver her wherever she needs to go. Lord knows I'm paying him enough for the little work he does.''

Belle burst into the room, saw her great-aunt and grinned broadly. ''Aunt Isabelle! What are you doing here?''

''I'm on my way to the beauty parlor, my dear, but I came to tell your mother about a wonderful opportunity for you.''

Belle's already-animated face perked up. She looked from her mother to her aunt.

''Donovan Delaney—I believe you've met him—has agreed to take you under his wing from time to time while he's working around town this summer. Sort of a junior apprenticeship.''

''Really! Oh, wow! Is this too cool or what, Mom?'' Belle cried, racing across the room to give Isabelle a hug.

Isabelle smiled benignly at Lara over the top of Belle's head. Lara had no choice but to smile back. She knew manipulation when she saw it. She still hadn't given her permission for Belle to spend time with Donovan, but if she didn't now, she'd seem like the Wicked Witch of the West. Sometimes, she thought, discretion really was the better part of valor.

''Yeah,'' she managed to say. ''Cool.''

Before finally departing for her twice-weekly hair appointment, Isabelle explained that Belle should call Donovan and make arrangements to meet him the next day. When Belle went upstairs to do that, Lara went into the kitchen, poured herself another cup of coffee and sat down at the table to think about her conversation with her aunt.

Isabelle knew something about Lara's and Donovan's relationship. But what? How much? And how

had she found out? The jailer had told her dad about
her visits and phone calls to Donovan, which was how
he coerced the truth from her. But she'd made him
promise not to tell anyone about Donovan, not even
Rowland, and her dad had been a man of his word,
even though he'd had plenty of other faults. And between him and Rowland Hardisty, they'd probably si-
lenced even the most talkative people in town. Her dad
had never been particularly close to Isabelle, who was
Lara's mother's aunt, so Lara couldn't see them en-
gaging in confidences. Which left Ruby Delaney. The
two women had grown close during the time Ruby had
cleaned house for Isabelle. Was it possible that Ruby
had confided in her boss?

"No." Lara said the word aloud. Donovan wouldn't
have told his mother the two of them were dating. He
wouldn't have told anyone. Then how had Isabelle
found out? Lara was tempted to ask her, but wasn't
sure she was up for it. She'd kept the lid to that particular Pandora's box shut for too many years to have
it opened now.

She knew her great-aunt was right about one thing,
though. It was time she granted Donovan forgiveness
for his behavior seventeen years ago. Deep down in
her heart she knew that he'd refused to see her to save
her from gossip and embarrassment. He was so con-
scious of his background that he hadn't wanted her to
be humiliated by their dating, so it followed that he
would be even more adamant about her not having to
deal with having a boyfriend who was being sent to
prison.

She'd known, but knowing hadn't eased her pain. It
was only as she'd grown older that she fully realized
what an unselfish thing he'd done, and even then she'd

clung to her bitterness, because it made facing the truth of her feelings harder.

As she'd admitted to herself the day she'd run into him at the school, she still felt something for Donovan Delaney. She'd known it since the day several weeks ago when he'd come to pick up Cassidy and she'd seen him looking over her back fence. Her heart had begun to beat fast and furiously, and her blood had begun to race as a hot flush of awareness spread throughout her body.

As corny as it sounded, the sky had seemed bluer and the birds had sung more sweetly. Emotions had chased each other through her, one behind the other. Joy, sorrow, desire, a bittersweet longing for something lost, and a resurgence of pain so sharp it could only mean her feelings were undoubtedly, indisputably, love. Lara had never seen any emotions that could make a person as happy or as miserable as love.

She'd combatted the knowledge as best she could, relying on her sharp tongue and a condescending manner to keep the feelings from overwhelming her. She must have overdone it, because Wes had called her on the carpet for her rude behavior.

Then, when she'd happened to run into Donovan at the school the other day, she hadn't had much time to rally her defenses. Besides, she doubted if many women could muster much of a defense against Donovan Delaney in tight jeans and a T-shirt. As impossible as it seemed, he looked even better now than he had in his youth. He was bigger and burlier than she remembered, but there wasn't an ounce of fat on him. He was fit, trim, with the kind of muscles earned by hours of physical labor and a grown man's maturity.

He looked good. Great. So wonderful that she'd come home and cried for all they'd lost.

As Isabelle had pointed out, Donovan had grown into a special person, and in spite of the hand life had dealt him, he appeared to have come through it all with his positive outlook intact, which, she thought, was no less a miracle than the wonders he'd shown her in the garden.

His coming into her life back then had been a miracle in itself, as had the realization that she was expecting his baby. She'd known the prospect of a baby would throw their carefully made plans into disarray, which had made her as frightened as she was excited, but never in her wildest dreams had she doubted that Donovan would want their child. She'd often wondered whether knowing about the baby would have made any difference in the stand he'd taken—which was immaterial now.

And, just as that made no difference, neither did the fact that she still loved him. She wasn't an insecure girl anymore. She was a woman with a college degree and a prominent position in town. A mother. She was divorced, for heaven's sake! Didn't that prove that she'd lost her naiveté? Besides, she was nobody's fool. Working with kids had taught her that. Someone might fool her once, but it seldom happened the second time. Attracted to him or not, she had no intention of letting Donovan Delaney get close enough to hurt her again. She had standards. Principles. And no desire to be made a fool of the second time.

Later that evening Belle was upstairs waiting for her father, who was picking her up and taking her to a movie. Lara had had a particularly rough day at summer school. A tussle had broken out between two al-most-twelfth-graders over a girl. She solved the alter-cation by threatening to expel all three, which would jeopardize their chances of graduating with the rest of the class the following June. A student had fallen in the gym and broken an ankle, and one of the air-conditioning units had wheezed its last breath with no chance of resuscitation.

She'd come home tired, cranky and looking forward to a long shower and a quiet evening in front of the television with a small glass of wine to take the edge off her mood and her frustrations. Her plan was thwarted by the parent of one of the students, who had called and talked for more than an hour. Then one of the neighbors had come over to chitchat, and before Lara knew it, it was past six o'clock and she hadn't yet had time to indulge herself.

Finally, she thought, stepping into the steaming shower cubicle. The shower was heavenly, and she stayed until the water ran cold. She patted herself dry and bundled her wet head in a fluffy white towel, hes-itating a moment before bypassing her usual terry cloth robe and padding naked to her closet. Occasionally when she felt a little sorry for herself and thought she needed a bit of pampering, she put on the pricey red silk robe Reed had given her the Christmas before their divorce. Pulling it from the padded hanger, she slipped her arms inside and wrapped it around her still-damp body.

She loved the way the silk felt against her skin, rev-eled in the brush of it against her thighs and the sen-suous caress of the fabric against her unbound breasts. It made her feel sexy and desirable, something she hadn't felt in more years than she could remember. It also made her excruciatingly aware of the length of her abstinence. She knew her sudden hedonistic yearning was tied to Donovan's return, but she refused to think about that, as if refusing to acknowledge it might make it go away.

As Lara passed Belle's room, she heard the muted sound of her television. No television for her, Lara thought. She would put Yanni and Kenny G on the CD player, pour herself a glass of vermouth, open the French doors that led to the patio and enjoy the sounds of summer.

She put on the music, poured the wine, opened the doors and stepped outside. It was still daylight, but the setting sun made the trees cast long shadows across the lawn. The face of the pool was quiet, and a dozen pink mandevilla blossoms lay on its surface, probably put there by Belle who loved the look of flowers floating in the water.

Glass in hand, Lara was crossing the rock patio when a movement to her left caused her to jump. A man stood on the far side of the pool near the photinias, his back to her, a plastic container in one hand and a wand of some sort in the other. It took only a few seconds for her to make the connection, but it wasn't the paraphernalia that tipped her off. It was the breadth of his shoulders and the narrowness of his hips beneath his formfitting T-shirt and jeans.

She must have made some sound, because he turned, and Lara saw that he was holding a sprayer. He'd been doing something to her diseased photinias, she realized on the level of her brain that was still in a functioning mode. The rest of her was engaged in total and complete reaction to the fact that he was there, within yards of her, and she was all but naked. Nerve endings and senses that had lain dormant for many years sprang to vibrant life.

He smiled. "Hi."

"What are you doing here?" she asked, casting a frowning glance at the wooden gate.

"I came to treat your shrubs," he said, cocking his head toward the red-tipped hedge. "I rang the bell, but no one answered." His hot gaze swept her from her bare feet to the top of her turban-wrapped head, lingering on the gentle thrust of her bare breasts beneath the tissue-paper silk. A slow smile of appreciation spread across his face, and her heart went into a kamikaze dive. "I guess you were in the shower."

Lara's body reacted accordingly, her breasts tightening and tingling in sudden embarrassing awareness. Her free hand clutched the lapels of her robe. "Belle was watching television, and something's wrong with the doorbell," she said to cover her sudden confusion. She noticed that her voice was low and breathless, unprofessional sounding, nothing like the voice of a high school principal. "It's hard to hear upstairs."

They stood there, in a silence that expanded along with an overwhelming, mutual awareness. Finally, as if he realized that someone should do something, Donovan set the spray rig down. "It was unlocked," he said, crossing his arms over his chest.

"What?" she asked. The spell was broken, but she had no idea what he was talking about.

"The gate. It was unlocked. I brought your trash can back inside."

Lara realized that Belle must have left the gate unlocked when she'd rolled out the garbage can that morning. "Oh." She stared at him for a moment and said, "I didn't ask you to come see to the shrubs."

"I know, but I was in the neighborhood." He shrugged. "There's no charge."

"It isn't that, it's just that it's…a bit unsettling to walk out into your backyard and find a stranger there."

His gaze made another leisurely journey over her body. She wondered suddenly if the sunlight made the delicate fabric transparent and wished she'd put on a pair of the underwear he'd taunted her about at the school.

"I'm hardly a stranger, Lara," he said, rounding the end of the pool and moving to within a few feet of her. "I'd even go so far as to say we were pretty close, once."

His mentioning of the past snapped the taut thread of awareness stretching between them. Memory of the pain she'd felt swamped the delicate feelings of longing and tenderness unfurling inside her. Distress edged her voice. "I thought so, too," she said, "but sometimes we find out we don't know people as well as we might think."

He took a step nearer. "I know I hurt you, but—"

"Don't!" she said, releasing her death grip on her robe and holding up her hand to keep him away. "Just…don't. After all this time, it doesn't matter anymore."

"It matters," he said, flatly. "It matters a lot, and we both know it. I'd like to have the chance to explain."

She closed her eyes against the pleading in his, trying her best to dredge up some resistance. When she opened them, he was still standing there, his hands tucked in his back pockets, his brooding gaze focused on her face.

"I figured out your reasons a long time ago, Donovan, but it didn't help at the time."

"I know, and I'm sorry."

She shook her head, her face was molded with earnest entreaty. "Why did you come back here?" she asked in a harsh whisper that betrayed how close she was to tears. "Why, after all these years?"

"Do you want the truth?" he asked, his blue eyes dancing with a reckless intensity.

"Of course I want the truth."

"You," he said, without the slightest trace of apology or embarrassment. "I came back because of you."

Chapter Three

The first thing Reed saw when he pulled onto Lara's street to pick up Belle was Donovan Delaney's work truck sitting at the curb. Lara must have decided to get something done about those hedges in the back. Reed shot back his cuff and checked the time. Just past six-thirty. A little late, but he supposed the people in seasonal work had to make hay while the sun was shining, as the old saying went. Good. It would give Reed a chance to check with Donovan and see if he was still okay with picking up Sophie and Cassidy from the airport on Friday.

Reed found the front door unlocked, something he'd cautioned Lara about several times, telling her times were changing. She said she'd never had to lock her door during the day, and she didn't intend to start now. He sighed. She was a headstrong woman.

He paused at the base of the stairs. Belle's television

was blaring. He decided to wait until he'd spoken with Lara before letting Belle know he'd arrived. This time of day, Lara was probably in the kitchen making dinner. Reed made his way through the house to the kitchen with its cherry wood cabinets, beaded lumber ceiling and profusion of green houseplants. A copper ceiling fan hung from the twelve-foot ceiling, circling slowly. There was no sign of Lara.

A bottle of vermouth—her favorite wine, though she seldom indulged in any kind of alcohol—sat on the counter. He smiled. Bad day. One of the doors to the back stood ajar, even though the air-conditioning was breathing cool air into the room. She must have gone outside to talk to Donovan. Reed crossed the room and started to let himself out through the partially open door, but something in the body language of the two people standing at the pool's edge stopped him.

Lara, barefoot and wearing the red silk robe he'd given her several years before, stood with her back to him, talking to Donovan who stood on the far side of the pool. As Reed watched, Donovan set down his spray equipment and came around the edge of the pool, stopping within a few feet of Lara, whose body seemed unnaturally rigid. Donovan faced Reed. Donovan seemed upset about something, and the look on his face was one of pure what? Longing?

Before Reed could do more than realize that the whole scenario was troubling somehow, Donovan took a step closer, and Lara held out her hand to stop him. Sudden comprehension drove the air from Reed's lungs. His hand tightened on the doorknob.

While his mind tried to process the information his eyes were recording, he saw Donovan stick his hands in his back pockets, as if he needed to do something

with them and wasn't sure what. Lara gave a violent
shake of her head and turned away from him, toward
the house. With desperation etched on his face, Donovan reached out and grabbed her upper arm, spinning
her around so quickly that the wine in the glass she
carried sloshed over the rim. From inside the house,
Reed couldn't hear what Donovan was saying, but it
wasn't hard to read his lips. *I love you, Lara. I never
stopped.*

Reed's head spun crazily. *Donovan and Lara.* It all
made sense now. Lara's despondency when they'd
married. Her willingness to let her father and his shape
her future. The baby. Dear sweet heaven! Reed
thought, as realization came crashing in around him.
The baby Lara had been carrying when they married
had been Donovan's. Reed would bet his not incon-
siderable bank account on it.

Trembling, Lara looked up into Donovan's eyes. He
wasn't hurting her; in fact, his grip on her arm was
surprisingly gentle. The weakness of her limbs was a
direct result of his touching her. It had been this way
from the very first time he'd cupped her chin in his
hand and kissed her, and she had the sinking feeling
that she would feel the same way when she drew her
last breath.

Even as the thought slipped through her mind, he
released his hold on her arm and reached up to take
her chin in his hand. His fingertips were rough from
hard work and as gentle as the brush of a butterfly's
wing. Their gazes clung to each other's, and Lara
heard her heart pounding out a slow, sluggish rhythm,
as if it, as she was, was waiting....

The pad of his thumb made a soft sweep of her

lower lip, and his fingers followed, tracing the shape of her mouth, while his eyes probed the troubled depths of hers. As she watched, he closed his eyes, as if the sight of her were too much. When he opened them, there was pleading there. And determination.

"Don't try to shut me out, Lara," he said. "I won't let you. It's time for us now."

Lara groaned and shook her head. As much as she wanted it, as much as she wanted him, she couldn't let him manipulate her so easily. "There is no us, Donovan. You saw to that when they put you in jail and you wouldn't see me."

"You know why I did that," he said in a low, earnest voice.

"I know. As a mature adult I can appreciate the gesture, but at eighteen it hurt unbearably. But it was a long time ago. Whatever it was that we felt for each other is over."

"Is it?"

"Yes!" The affirmation was spoken with far more conviction than she felt.

"You have no feelings for me." It was a statement, not a question.

"I think you're a fine man, who's overcome a lot of adversity."

Donovan swore, telling her exactly what she could do with her assessment of him. "And you don't feel anything for me? No love? Not even desire?"

"No." A whisper.

He released his hold on her chin and let his fingertips trail down her throat to the deep vee where the lapels of her robe overlapped. His gaze followed. Lara felt her breasts grow heavy and full, while, contrarily, the tips hardened in sudden desire.

"You're a liar, Lara." He stepped back a step and offered her a half smile. "But that's okay. I lied to myself for a long time, too."

Without another word he turned and walked away, retracing his steps around the pool. Lara watched as he picked up his sprayer and let himself out the gate. He never once turned back to see if she was still there. He must have known she was.

Reed, who'd witnessed the whole encounter, watched Donovan gather his things and leave, watched the starch go out of Lara's spine when he did. Watched as she put the wineglass to her mouth, tipped back her head and downed the contents in one long gulp. Then, shoulders drooping, she turned and headed back toward the house. Reed retreated into the room, so he wouldn't be the first thing she saw when she came inside. So she wouldn't know he'd seen everything that had transpired between her and Donovan. Unfortunately, the first words out of Reed's mouth nullified his plan.

"So it was Donovan Delaney," he said, the moment Lara closed the door.

She gasped. "What are you doing here?" she asked, ignoring the question.

"I came to pick up our daughter, or had you forgotten I was taking her to the movies?"

"No. I hadn't forgotten." But clearly she had, at least momentarily. She looked at her empty glass, and Reed reached for the bottle, deciding another wouldn't hurt her, and refilled the glass.

"The baby was Donovan's, wasn't it?" he asked, careful to make his tone unconfrontational. Thank God he had no need to feel threatened or judgmental. Their relationship had evolved to that of good and trusted friends.

"Yes." The eyes Lara raised to his were filled with shame, remorse, uncertainty. To his horror they glazed over with tears. He'd seldom seen her cry, in all the years they were together. He didn't go to her, didn't offer her any comfort in his arms. She wouldn't like that. "Why didn't you tell me?" he asked instead. "Especially after you found out about Sophie?"

"I was too hurt and angry at Donovan at first. Then, after I lost the baby, I was grieving...." She slid onto the barstool across the counter from him.

"I remember." He would never forget the depth of her pain and how powerless he'd been to comfort her.

"I didn't want to burden you. I knew you were hurting about something yourself, and I believed I deserved it, somehow. Later, when you and I decided that we'd make our marriage a real one, the timing didn't seem right. I thought if I ignored it, pretended it never happened, maybe it would all just...go away."

"How long had you been seeing him before they arrested him?"

"Several months. But we'd been fighting the attraction for at least a year before that." A fleeting half smile flickered across her lips. "I had a hard time convincing him to see me at all. He didn't want me to be embarrassed by him. As if I could be," she added.

"So you and Donovan were doing the same thing Sophie and I and Wes and Justine were doing, huh?"

Shock filled Lara's eyes. "Wes and Justine?" she repeated. "My brother dated Justine Sutton?"

Instantly Reed regretted the thoughtless comment. "I guess he never said anything."

"No. How did the two of them ever get together?"

"She and Sophie had a reputation for being easy back then, and like the spoiled, arrogant rich kids we were, Wes and I decided to see if the rumors were true. We double-dated the first time we asked them out. It didn't take long for me to find out that the rumors about Sophie were lies. I can't speak for Justine. All I know is that your brother saw her until the day she packed up and left town. It tore him up."

"Justine Sutton leaving town tore up Wes?" Lara asked, unable to hide her shock. "You're kidding, right?"

"No. And don't think you're going to get off the hook so easily.

"What do you mean?"

Reed smiled. "You aren't going to get out of telling me everything about you and Donovan by changing the subject to Wes." He held up the bottle. "More?"

"No, thanks. I've had more than enough." She sighed. "What else is there to say? We loved each other, we were sleeping together, but we were being very careful, or so we thought. We had a plan. Donovan was taking classes at the community college, and he'd applied for a grant and some loans so he could go to the university in Fayetteville. He wanted to get his degree before we told anyone we were seeing each other."

"That's commendable."

"Yes, well, it may surprise you, but Donovan is a very conscientious person with very high standards. He's also very sensitive about his background. He didn't want me embarrassed by him or his family. He wanted to—as he put it—bring something worthwhile to the marriage. He wanted my father to know he could support me, and he wanted me to be able to hold my head up when someone asked who I was marrying.''

''But 'The best-laid plans of mice and men,''' Reed quoted.

''Go to hell in a handbasket,'' Lara said, misquoting the famous line. ''He shot his dad and got sent to prison.''

''No, he didn't,'' Reed said, the words spilling out before he could stop them.

Lara frowned. ''I beg your pardon.''

Wishing he could call them back, knowing he shouldn't have said anything until he talked with Sophie about sharing the truth with Lara, Reed had no choice but to forge ahead. Somehow he felt Sophie would understand, especially if she knew about her brother and Lara.

''If I tell you something you have to promise not to say a word to anyone. Ever.''

The confusion in Lara's eyes deepened. She sketched a hasty *X* over her heart. ''Promise.''

''No, I mean it, Lara,'' he said in the voice he used to intimidate witnesses and juries. ''You can never speak of this to anyone outside the two of us, Sophie and Donovan. Not as long as you're breathing.''

''You're scaring me, Reed,'' Lara said, her eyes wide.

''I hope so. It's literally a matter of life and death.''

''Life and death,'' she echoed. ''Whose?''

''Sophie's. Mine. And yours and Donovan's if you ever hope to have a life with him.''

Lara blew out a harsh breath. ''Okay. You've made a believer out of me. I promise. I swear. Do you want me to write it in blood?''

Reed realized he'd come on pretty strong, but he

hadn't just found Sophie to have her taken away from him by some warped justice system, if anyone found out the truth.

"Donovan didn't shoot Hutch that night. Sophie did."

"What!"

Reed nodded. "She'd refused to have an abortion, and Hutch was…beating her, trying to hit her in the stomach, so she would lose the baby. She managed to get away and got the shotgun down. She told him to stay back. He rushed her and she pulled the trigger. Donovan came in and saw what had happened. He knew she was pregnant and that she wasn't up to serving jail time."

"But wouldn't the shooting have been self-defense or justifiable homicide or something like that?"

"Yeah," Reed said. "But you have to remember that we're talking about sixteen- and eighteen-year-olds. Sophie was in shock, and Donovan was scared to death. Neither of them was thinking too clearly. They weren't that familiar with the law, except to know the Delaneys were usually on the wrong side of it."

"Dear God!"

Reed went on to tell Lara how Donovan insisted Sophie hide the money her father had extorted from Rowland Hardisty—or as Hutch's version went, money Rowland offered so Sophie could leave town and start a new life. He even told her how Sophie's conscience had begun to prick her when news of Cassidy's paternity had come out a few weeks ago and how she'd called Sheriff Lawrence and told him the truth.

"What did Micah say?" Lara asked, spellbound by what Reed was telling her.

"He told her that as far as he was concerned, Donovan had paid for the crime and there was no sense bringing it all up again."

"I always knew Micah Lawrence was a good man," Lara said softly. Silence filled the room as the weight of Reed's disclosure settled over them.

"Did Donovan know about the baby?" Reed asked after several long, quiet seconds.

Lara's hands lay knotted together on top of the counter, her knuckles white. "No. I found out a few days after the arrest. I went to the jail, but he wouldn't see me. I called, but he wouldn't take my calls. I wrote, and he sent the letters back, unopened. The jailer told dad, and he managed to get the truth about Donovan and the baby out of me. You know the rest."

Reed leaned across the counter and covered her hands with both of his. She curled her fingers around his and gripped hard. Their eyes, wet with unshed tears, met. Reed offered her a tender smile. "Yeah. I know the rest. I think the two of us have done pretty well by each other, all things considered."

Lara smiled back. "Me, too."

"So, do you think there's a chance for you and Donovan?"

One of Lara's silk-clad shoulders lifted in a half-hearted shrug. "A lot of time has passed. As sad as it makes me to think about what we were cheated of, and how much I might wonder what we lost and if we'd have been happy together, I know we can't turn back time. People change. Neither Donovan nor I are the people we were back then."

"That's what Sophie and I are finding out."

"And?"

"I like some of the changes in her, and others I don't. She was always strong, but now she's...I don't know...tougher than she used to be. She feels the same way about me. But even when people are married for years, they change, and the marriage has to adapt to those changes."

"That sounds like a bunch of psychologist mumbo jumbo to me," Lara said, smiling.

"Maybe. But it's true. The bottom line is whether or not you care for the person and if you're committed to the relationship. We are."

"It isn't the same, though, is it?"

"Good grief, no!" Reed said with a soft laugh. "It's different, because we're different. In some ways it's better. Much better."

"I'm happy for you, Reed," Lara told him, sincerity shining in her dark eyes.

"It's there for you, too."

"Do you really think so?"

"Remember what you told me at the Woodcutters' Festival after you saw me with Sophie and figured out the flame was still burning?"

"What?"

"You said that whatever it was we felt for each other hadn't gone away and that maybe there was enough of a spark to be fanned into a bigger flame, but that we'd never know if we didn't pursue it. Well, from what I just saw out there by the pool, that flame hasn't gone out for you and Donovan, either."

"You saw us?"

"Yeah. Not that there was much to see." When she didn't say anything, he said, "Your advice was sound, Lara. I'm advising you to take it."

* * *

When Reed and Belle left, Lara locked up, switched her drink of choice to instant cappuccino and went back outside. This time she saw nothing in the beauty of the backyard, heard no summer nighttime sounds. This time she was consumed with the news Reed had told her. Donovan. Innocent. Paying for a crime he didn't commit to protect the sister he loved and the baby she was carrying.

Tears began to slide down her cheeks, slowly at first, then faster and harder, tears accompanied by deep gulping breaths and harsh sobs. She cried for all that Sophie and Donovan must have gone through growing up. Cried for the lost love of a very good man and for a baby, gone before it had a chance. She cried for lost innocence and teenagers in general, marveling at how any of them turned out okay when they faced very adult situations with raging hormones, immaturity and an inclination to kick authority in the teeth. All this with parents who, for the most part, meant well and wanted to protect them from pain, but who often made the wrong decisions themselves.

What was it Isabelle used to always say? Oh, yeah. Kids were like pancakes. You ought to throw the first one out. And kids should be born eighteen-years-old and ready to leave home. The problem was that even at eighteen most of them weren't ready. Not really. Of course, Lara knew that it was the actual leaving and dealing with the problems that came their way that made them grow up.

She remembered how she and Reed had packed up and moved so he could be near the university and away from Rowland and how unprepared they were for marriage. It had been one of the most difficult times of her life. She and Reed were both so wrapped up in their personal tragedies that they hadn't even leaned on each other the way most newlyweds would. They'd struggled alone with the changes in their lives, and then she'd lost Donovan's baby, and nothing but her misery had mattered for a very long time.

To give him credit, Reed had done his best to console her, but nothing and no one could ease her pain, a pain she was experiencing all over again, now that she knew the truth behind Donovan's rejection, a truth that made her even more sorrowful for what she'd lost. She thought of what Reed said, and wondered if he was right. Should she give the feelings she still felt for Donovan a chance?

Belle had gone to visit her grandmother, and Reed was in the kitchen of the small apartment located at the back of his parents' house, fixing himself and Belle a frozen pizza and thinking about his conversation with Lara. Never in a thousand years would he have guessed that the man in his ex-wife's past was Donovan Delaney. Which is probably how most of the people in town felt when they learned he was marrying Sophie. The comparison brought his thoughts to his dad and the widening chasm between them.

Reed and Rowland hadn't spoken much since their argument over the events that had sent Sophie away from Lewiston—Hutch's version of the truth versus Rowland's. Reed knew Sophie was right when she said that both of their fathers had lied, and that none of it mattered now that they were in possession of the truths that mattered.

It didn't matter whether the money Sophie used to leave town was blackmail money Hutch had extorted from Rowland in exchange for not going to the authorities with the lie that Reed had raped Sophie or whether Rowland had offered it freely so Sophie could get an abortion and leave town to find a new life. It was over. Done. What mattered was that Reed had found out about Cassidy, and since his announcement that he was marrying Sophie, he and his father, who'd always had a rocky relationship, had spoken nothing but the most basic words. Celeste, Reed's mother, who was having a hard time with the news herself, was at least willing to give Sophie a chance, mostly because of Cassidy.

Though the truth of the incident the night Hutch was killed had been sworn to secrecy between Donovan, Sophie and Reed, Cassidy had been told that Rowland was opposed to the relationship between her parents and that he had given Sophie the money that had enabled her to leave town and start over. Neither Sophie nor Reed had thought any good could be served by telling her that her other grandfather had wanted her dead.

Rowland had always had a need for control, which was why, as a promising young surgeon, he had chosen to practice general medicine in a small town instead of moving his family to a larger city. It was better to be the big fish in a small pond than the other way around.

Rowland was good at what he did, and he knew it, and to this day he received several offers a year to work on staff at some of the most prestigious hospitals in the country. People came from across the state to have him as their surgeon, and because of the family money and the fees Rowland charged, Lewiston boasted operating facilities to rival any in the state.

The problem was that Rowland tried to control the

lives of everyone around him, which tended to alienate people. Reed's mother, eclipsed by her husband's domineering personality for almost forty years, was a good and quiet woman. Too good for his father, in Reed's opinion. Reed knew about his dad's affair with his nurse, and hated that his mother had to put up with the outrage—if she knew. Of course it wasn't Rowland's first affair, and Reed doubted it would be his last, but he hated that his mother had wasted her life being Rowland's dupe.

A peremptory knock sounded at the door, a knock Reed knew well. It was almost as if thinking of his dad had conjured him up. Reed slid the pizza into the hot oven and set the timer.

"Come in."

Rowland, dressed in what passed for casual clothes in high-end circles, strolled into the small house and settled himself on a bar stool. "I can't believe you're really going to do it," he said without even a proper greeting.

"I can't believe you are, either," Reed shot back as he stuck a small enamel pan beneath the running water.

"What?" Rowland asked, frowning.

"I can't believe you're going to start in on me about my marrying Sophie. It's happening, Dad. Seventeen years too late, but it's happening. My advice to you is to get over it. Sophie may not have been born to the most impressive family, but somehow her mother managed to bring her and her brother up to be responsible, well-adjusted, caring adults. And believe me, she bleeds the same way you and I do."

Rowland didn't reply.

"If you could get past your preconceived notions, you might like her. She's smart and wise and very good at what she does. You, of all people, should respect that. As a matter of fact, the two of you would probably have a lot to talk about, if you'd just give yourself a chance to get to know her."

"I can't imagine myself carrying on a conversation with Sophie Delaney."

"Sophie Carlisle," Reed corrected. "Widow of a highly successful investment banker. Ph.D in psychology, owner of a successful practice. Mother of an incredibly beautiful, incredibly bright sixteen-year-old who just happens to be your granddaughter."

Reed paused for breath and to regroup his thoughts. "You know, Dad, perspective is a very important thing. Sometimes, as they say, we can't see the forest for the trees."

"Meaning?"

"Meaning that if you were a young man, I wouldn't want either of my daughters dating or marrying *you.*"

A shocked look passed over Rowland's face. "And why not? I'm from a good family, have money and am very successful."

"You're also selfish, manipulative, condescending and controlling. Despite your affairs, you have no real passion for anything but your work, and any compassion you may have is directed toward your patients. And when I think about it, I'm not so sure that's genuine or if you hope for their speedy recovery so you can add another success to the score sheet."

Rowland's face looked pale, but he managed a sarcastic smile. "Why don't you tell me how you really feel about me, Reed?"

"What's the matter? Like to dish it out but can't take it, Dad? You want more? Okay. How about this? You're my father, and I love you, but I don't like you

very much. I think my mother is too good for you.
You've treated her like garbage for as long as I can
remember, and she deserves better."

"Your mother and I are none of your business."

"Then Sophie and I are none of yours. You can't
have it both ways. At least stop flaunting your affairs
for the whole town to see. You should at least have
enough respect for her to be discreet."

Reed paused again, staring at his father's stony features.

"Are you finished?" Rowland asked, getting to his
feet.

Reed threw his hands into the air. "Yeah, I'm finished. I don't know why I bother."

Rowland ignored the comment and headed for the
back door. "I'll come back when you're in a better
frame of mind."

"Dad," Reed said as Rowland opened the door. He
paused, but didn't turn around. "Are you coming to
the wedding?" Reed saw the sudden stiffening of his
father's spine. Rowland turned.

"Oh, I'll be there," he said with a thin smile. "If
you really go through with it. In spite of my many
faults, and evidently they're legion, I have at least a
veneer of propriety, and it would reflect badly if I
failed to attend my only child's wedding."

The stuffy statement was classic Rowland, Reed
thought, as his dad shut the door, but it did ease his
mind. He wanted his dad at the wedding to show public support of the marriage.

Reed dropped some tea bags into the boiling water.
The timer rang, and he pulled the pizza from the oven.
He wished there was some way to make Rowland for-
get the past and see Sophie for what she was. Reed

supposed he should be thankful for small favors. As much as he might be against the marriage, Rowland would never let anyone outside the family know his true feelings. The "veneer of propriety" he claimed would enable him to put up a good front to the world. Only those closest to him would suffer his true feelings.

The next morning Donovan attacked the flower bed at the Echolses' house with a vengeance. He was still feeling pretty raw from his encounter with Lara. He'd hardly slept. Instead, fueled by the recent memory of her—haughty and wary of him in the scarlet robe, he'd tormented himself with the precious memories of her as she'd been in the past. Innocent. Hungry. Passionate.

Donovan used the spade to loosen the soil around a maverick privet hedge that had homesteaded in a patch of day lilies, then grabbed it and pulled it from the ground.

"That's privet, right?"

Belle. Great. He'd been so wrapped up in his thoughts he'd forgotten that she'd called to thank him for offering to teach her more about plants and say she'd be joining him this morning. This was just what he needed to make his day complete. A constant reminder of Lara and all they'd lost.

"Right," he said, straightening and summoning a smile. She was a cute kid who looked a lot like her mother. Donovan stifled a sudden surge of jealousy that this child was Reed's. She should have been his. "Privet can be a problem."

"Aunt Isabelle says it's evasive," Belle said.

Donovan bit back a grin. "That's *invasive*. It means

that if you don't take measures to keep it under control, the plant will run rampant."

"I know what invasive means," she said, a bit testily. "But somehow I always say the wrong one." She slanted a look up and sideways from the corner of her eyes. "I do know the difference between prostrate and prostate."

Donovan turned away to pick up the shovel and hide a smile. Kids. "That's a good thing to know when you're in the plant business."

"Men have prostates—you know, those—"

"Yeah, I know," Donovan interrupted.

"And plants that don't grow tall—that grow flat and cover the ground are prostrate."

"You got it. Why don't you take this spade and dig up the bulbs in the little round bed over there."

"Dig? I thought you were going to teach me about horticulture. What is digging going to teach me?"

"A work ethic for a start. You have to dig to plant. It isn't all fun. As a matter of fact, gardening and yard work are two of the most physically challenging things there are to do."

She rolled her eyes, turned away and started toward the bed of wilted hyacinths. "Oh, look!" she cried, pointing to another bed. "Mrs. Echols has an herb garden. I just love the lamb's ears, don't you? They're so soft. I like the wooly thyme, too."

"All the herbs are great plants in one way or the other," Donovan said. "Did you know that in the south a lot of them are perennial?"

"I didn't know that." She pointed a finger at him and said, "Mint."

"Mint?" he repeated, having no idea what she was talking about.

"It's—" she closed her eyes and thought a moment "—very invasive."

Donovan smiled. "Give the girl a blue ribbon."

Belle smiled back. "Do you know anything about the language of flowers?"

"I know rosemary is for remembrance," he said. "That's about it."

"Tell you what," Belle said. "You teach me about plants and I'll teach you about the language of flowers. Deal?"

Donovan looked down into the face of the girl whose mother he loved more than life itself. She was at that awkward, in-between age. No longer a child. Not yet a woman. She'd be a beauty one day, though. Just like her mother. The promise was in her bone structure, the classic shape of her nose and the elegant bow of her lips. It occurred to him again, that this child—no, not this child, but one similar and just as precious—could have been his. Should have been.

He reined in his thoughts before they got out of hand. There was no use wallowing in regrets and what might have been. Or what might be, for that matter. The only thing he had any kind of control over was the present. He used to love spending time with his niece, Cassidy, but she was growing up and away from him and her mother. Sharing his knowledge with Belle would help fill the void left by Cassidy's maturing.

Though he could have cared less about the language of flowers, in that one bittersweet moment he couldn't have refused Belle anything. He stuck out his hand, and she put hers in it. They shook, vigorously.

"Deal," he said.

The sealing of the bargain brought a moment's panic that he squelched. He'd agreed to this junior apprenticeship solely to please Isabelle Duncan and had viewed it as something to be borne until school started. Now he began to think that maybe it might not be too bad.

Chapter Four

Three hours later, it was time to call it a day. Belle put the shovel she'd been using into the back of the truck and swiped her forearm across her sweaty face, making a muddy smear. "So," she asked, "how'd I do?"

Donovan pulled the bandanna he kept in his back pocket out and handed it to her. What was a little sweat between friends? "You did real good," he told her. "For a girl."

Her mouth fell open and snapped shut. "Sexist pig!"

It sounded so much like something she'd heard Lara say it was all Donovan could do to keep from laughing. He *tsked* softly. "Is that any way to talk to your boss?"

He saw the fear enter her eyes and decided he'd

teased her enough. He laughed. "I was just kidding. You did great. Did you learn anything?"

She nodded. "Raised beds are good for drainage. Mulch holds in water and keeps out weeds. Watering deep makes better root systems." Her shrug made her look older, wiser. "I'm too tired to think. Should I meet you back here in the morning? I don't have anything to do tomorrow, and this is better than sitting around watching TV."

Her genuine enthusiasm made Donovan regret that he had to tell her no. "Not tomorrow. Sophie and Cassidy are flying in, and your dad has court, so I have to drive to Little Rock and pick them up."

Her face fell. "Oh."

Donovan could hardly bear to see the disappointment in her eyes. He said, "What the heck," and followed that with "Would you like to go with me?"

"Can I?" she asked, her eyes widening with excitement. "I mean, may I?"

"That's up to your mom," Donovan told her. "But it looks like Sophie is going to be your stepmom, so you ought to spend some time getting to know her."

"Right," Belle said, falling right into the "reasoning" game. "I know she's your sister, so you might be biased," she said, "but is she gonna be good to my dad?"

"Biased?" Donovan asked, impressed by her vocabulary and evading the question momentarily.

"Yeah, biased. It means—"

"I know what it means," he said, picking up her bike and carrying it to the truck, "but what kind of word is that for a kid your age to use?"

Belle's frown turned into a smile when she saw that he was teasing again. "It's what happens to an otherwise normal child who has a mom who's an *educator*. What are you doing with my bike?''

He lifted the bicycle into the back of the one-ton flatbed and closed the tailgate to the makeshift wooden side rails he and Jett had made for it.

''I'm taking you home. You're tired, it's hot, and it isn't far out of my way. Besides, I need to ask your mom if you can go with me in the morning.''

Any excuse to see her.

''Cool,'' Belle said, her eyes brightening.

''Did we forget anything?'' he asked. ''That's another lesson. Good tools cost good money. You don't want to leave them behind, and you want to take care of them when you finish.''

Belle's gaze razed the area where they'd been working. ''It looks like we got everything.''

''Load up, then.'' She climbed into the cab beside him, and he started the engine.

They went a full block before she said, ''My grandfather said you were raised poor. Is that true?''

Donovan glanced over at her, meeting her gaze fully. ''Yep.''

''Was it terrible?''

''We had plenty to eat and a decent place to live. Not fancy, but clean and decent. We didn't have a lot of clothes. We didn't wear seventy-dollar tennis shoes, thirty-dollar T-shirts and we didn't get to go to the mall every weekend to hang out and spend money at the arcade. But there are a lot of things worse than not having money,'' he said.

''Like what?''

''Like not being happy and not having freedom.''

''Cassidy told me you'd been to jail,'' Belle said with brutal honesty. ''That you shot your own father.''

Well, this ought to put an end to the gardening lessons, Donovan thought. "That's right. He abused us. Not sexually. Physically."

Her face was pale, and she looked as if she wished she hadn't brought up the subject. "He beat you?"

"Regularly," Donovan said, determined not to compromise the truth any more than necessary to protect his sister. He'd tell Belle just enough of the truth and let her draw her own conclusions. "He was drunk and mad at Sophie. He tried to kill her."

Belle's eyes grew even wider, and her face paler. "Really?"

"Really." They drove another block in silence. Knowing it was time to change the subject, Donovan said, "The answer to your question is yes."

"Yes?" He could tell by the confusion in her eyes that they'd gotten so far from her original question that she had no idea what he was talking about.

"Yes, Sophie will be good to your dad. That doesn't mean they won't get mad at each other or that they won't argue, but she does love him. A lot. And she'll love you, too, if you'll let her."

"She won't be my mom."

"No. But she won't be the wicked stepmom, either. She's strict sometimes, but she won't ask you to do anything or behave in any way that she doesn't expect from Cassidy."

"That seems fair," Belle said after a moment's thought. "Cassidy is cool. I really like her, and I'm glad she's my sister."

Donovan smiled. "From what Cass says, the feeling's mutual."

Lara was moving the sprinkler in the front lawn when the truck pulled to a stop at the curb. Donovan!

She hadn't expected him to bring Belle home.

What would you have done if you'd known? Freshened your makeup and put on your best shorts outfit? Don't be a twit. Hastily she rubbed her dirty palms down the sides of her khaki shorts and smoothed back the hair that had escaped the scrunchie holding it out of her face.

Lara watched while Donovan got Belle's bike out of the truck, watched in amazement as Belle matched her steps to his as they came up the sidewalk toward her. She looked up at him, as if they shared a secret. Lara's heart gave a painful lurch. What kind of spell had he cast on her daughter, anyway? *No spell, Lara. He's just given her his time, shared his thoughts and been kind to her.* Simple things, and all that most kids wanted from the adults in their lives.

She summoned a smile and tried not to stare at the man she'd once shared the most intimate act with. "Hi."

"Hi," the duo said in unison.

"How'd it go?"

Donovan and Belle looked at each other. "Great," they said together. "Donovan let me dig up a flower bed," Belle said, as if he'd granted her her dearest wish.

"And got most of it on you from the looks of it," Lara said with a wry twist of her lips. She looked from one to the other and decided to cut to the chase. "What's going on?"

"I'm picking up Sophie and Cassidy at the airport in the morning," Donovan said. "I was wondering if Belle could go."

"Meaning she asked to go with you," Lara said, pinning her daughter with a warning look.

"Actually, she didn't." He smiled. "When I told her I wouldn't be working in the morning, she just looked up at me with those sad, puppy-dog eyes—" Belle shot him a dirty look "—and I broke under the pressure. But there are valid reasons she should go."

"Which are?"

"I need to get to know Sophie better," Belle said.

"Probably a good idea," Lara said, nodding. "And?"

"And I've really missed Cassidy, and I'm sick of being here by myself most of the day."

Guilt pricked Lara's heart. Summer was the time she and Belle should be spending more time together, but as principal, she had to be on hand during summer school.

"Those are definitely valid reasons," Lara said. She shifted her gaze from Belle's face to Donovan's. "Are you okay with this?"

"Sure."

"Then I have no problem with her going."

Belle's face brightened. "Thanks, Mom!" She gave Lara a hug and turned to Donovan as if she might do the same, but something stopped her, and she reached out to shake his hand, instead. "Thank you, Mr. Delaney."

Just as properly, Donovan accepted the handshake. "You're very welcome, Miss Hardisty. And call me Donovan."

Belle looked up at Lara who shot him a stern look. "That's up to Mr. Delaney."

"It's okay if you call me, Donovan, too, Mrs. Hardisty."

Seeing the heat smoldering in his eyes, Lara had a vivid recollection of herself seventeen years earlier, breathing heavily, quivering in the aftermath of a release so exquisite the pleasure was closely akin to pain. Remembered chanting his name over and over, a mantra against the harsh reality of the world outside her father's cabin on the lake, the place where they'd rendezvoused.

"All right," she said in a breathless voice. She turned to Belle in an effort to break the spell of the past. "Why don't you go up and take a shower? We're having dinner at Amy's."

"Okay." With a wave, Belle skipped up the walk to the house.

Donovan reached down, picked up the sprinkler and dragged it and the unwieldy hose to a new location. Muscles rippled in his arms, and a shiver of longing flickered inside her.

"A sprinkler system would eliminate all this."

"Drumming up business, Donovan?" she asked in a taunting tone.

He straightened, turned and planted his hands on his lean hips. "Picking another fight?" he countered. "Take it from one who knows. Manufactured anger is never a good defense against your true feelings."

She crossed her arms over her breasts. "I don't have to manufacture my anger at you. It's plenty real, and it's justified."

"Goodbye, Lara," he said, turning and starting for the truck.

She watched him go, her heart sinking. Why did she persist in bringing up the past? Why couldn't she just forget it?

Hating herself for not being able to let go, hating

him for letting her go, she taunted, "What's the matter, Donovan? Why don't you want to talk about the past? You said the other night that you came back because of me. Why? To try and establish some kind of new relationship?" She laughed, but it wasn't a pleasant sound. "Why should I, after the way you dumped me before?"

He stopped at the curb, stretched out his arms and rested his palms on the battered fender. Lara was breathing heavily, waiting for his next move, feeling the tears pool in her eyes and slide silently down her cheeks, waiting for him to answer, just as she'd waited for an answer from him so long ago….

Finally, he turned, raking a hand through his tousled hair. "I'd be glad to talk about the past, Lara, but you don't want to talk. You want to fight. You want to attack me for what I did, and you want to hear my defense. Then you're going to tell me I was wrong, even though you know I was right. Besides, you said you knew why I did what I did and you understand, so why don't you just let it go? Personally, I've had enough fighting to last the rest of my life."

Without waiting for an answer, he rounded the hood of the truck and got inside, firing the engine with a belch of smoke and pulling away from the curb with grinding gears.

Lara watched him go, sorrow sinking its talons deep into her heart. He'd finally put it into words. *You said you knew why I wouldn't see you….* Somehow that made it all the more real. Why did she persist in alienating him? What did she hope to prove?

She knew the answer to that, if she would only look deep enough and be honest with herself. She wanted a reason to be angry at him, because anger was her only defense against the feelings that grew each time she saw him. She groaned. How could she still care for him? How could she let a man who'd abandoned her back into her life? And how could she live in this town knowing she could run into him on any corner?

You could leave. Your résumé looks good, and there are other towns who'd be glad to have your knowledge and experience. Yes, she could leave, but she wouldn't. She couldn't take Belle away from Reed, and she couldn't leave her aunt. Her life—and until Donovan came back it was satisfactory—was here in Lewiston, and there was no way she could pull up stakes and start over somewhere new.

Lara turned and went to the front door, her spine straight, her shoulders back. She'd have to learn to ignore Donovan Delaney. She'd have to put her feelings aside and deal with him in a purely professional way. She slammed the door shut and bolted it, determined to seek some sort of normalcy where Donovan was concerned. But the image in her mind as she went up the stairs was of the way he looked after a hard day's work, all scruffy and dirty, his end-of-day beard a dark shadow on his lean cheeks, his dark hair finger and wind tossed, his blue eyes a startling, compelling blue.

She thought about his parting line, about having had enough fighting to last a lifetime, and felt a deep shame. She had no idea what he'd endured, and probably didn't want to know.

"You're going to have to deal with this, Donovan," Sophie said the next day after he'd told her about his most recent encounters with Lara. "Whether you like it or not."

Donovan had picked Sophie and Cassidy up and then brought them to one of his favorite Chinese places for lunch. Cassidy and Belle had gone off to check out the strip mall's other shops while Donovan and Sophie lingered over coffee.

"I don't want to fight with her," he said, repeating what he'd told Lara the day before. "I want to love her."

Sophie reached out and placed a hand over his, which held the handle of his coffee cup in a white-knuckled grip. "A festering wound won't heal."

He raised his gaze to hers. "Meaning?"

"Sometimes you have to open it up and let all the poison out. Meaning that you hurt her. No!" she said, holding up a hand to stop him from speaking. "I know you had your reasons, and Lara is a smart woman who says she knows what they were. If you asked her, she'd probably even admit that those reasons were logical, maybe even honorable. But the heart has no interest in logic and reason. It just feels. The bottom line is you hurt her, badly. At the time it was probably just a total feeling of rejection by the man she loved. But now, as an adult, she may read an even deeper meaning into it."

"Like what?" he asked, the emotions inside him feeling like a strange brew of irritation and bewilderment.

Sophie lifted one shoulder in a careless shrug. "Like you didn't believe in what the two of you had, enough to trust that she'd stand by you or that it could weather the kind of storm you knew was brewing."

"I loved her, Sophie," he said, determined to substantiate his stand on the issue. "Her family had a certain standing in the community. I didn't want people talking about her and her jailbird boyfriend. I didn't want her—" he struggled to find the right word "—tarnished by all the ugliness."

"I know that. *She* knows that. What you aren't grasping, brother dear, is that your reasons don't matter. Her feelings of rejection do. Believe me, the psyche can come up with some pretty bizarre rationalizations when you have years to speculate on why something did or didn't happen."

"So what are you telling me?"

"That you're going to have to stop stonewalling her. You're going to have to let her have her say. You don't have to argue. Just listen. And I mean listen. You'll hear exactly what's eating at her. Then see if there are enough pieces left of what you had to pick up and go on. See if you even want to."

"I want to. It's all I really do want."

He saw the concern in his sister's eyes and knew he didn't want to hear what she was about to say. "I know. But you have to come to terms with the fact that Lara may not want the same thing. You aren't Reed, and Lara isn't me. The situation is different."

"Different, but not worse."

"That isn't for me to say. What I am saying is that this story may not have a happy ending. Can you deal with that?"

A spasm of pain squeezed his heart. "Yeah. I can deal with it."

"And if she shows absolutely no sign of wanting to pick up where you left off, you'll move on and try to find someone else?"

"I'll try."

"That's all any of us can do," Sophie said. "I know you think there will never be anyone but Lara. But if the worst happens, and you get some true closure on it, if you know it will absolutely *not* happen, then you can heal and move on. I'm a prime example that it can happen.''

Donovan knew she was talking about how, when she'd left Lewiston pregnant with Reed's baby, she'd been heartbroken and disillusioned with him and life and how, both loving and hating Reed but certain that they could never be together, she'd met Jake Carlisle, a man she'd learned to love deeply. Their marriage had been one of near perfection until his death a little more than two years ago.

''I know it can happen,'' he said, hearing the weariness in his voice. ''I know I might find someone else, but the older I get, the less I believe it.''

Sophie shook her head and offered him a soft smile. ''All I can say is keep the faith.''

Donovan exhaled loudly. ''I'll do my best.'' He picked up the check. ''How much do I owe you for this little counseling session, Doc?''

''How about we take it out in landscaping?'' she said, smiling.

''Works for me.''

By Friday evening Lara was heartily sick of hearing what a fantastic time Belle had had on her outing with Donovan. He was so cool and wasn't he a hunk? Cassidy was the best, and Sophie was really nice. Belle didn't think she'd mind having her for a stepmom at all. Of course, she *knew* they wouldn't get along *all* the time, but she really thought it would be okay.

Lara had planned to take Belle shopping and to lunch the next day, but when Reed called and said Sophie wanted Belle to come along while they looked for a house, her enthusiastic "May I go, Mom, please, please, please?" told Lara that her own idea was, at best, second-rate.

She gave her consent and then wondered what she'd do with a free Saturday all alone. She was saved from total boredom by Isabelle, who called with a brunch invitation.

"It sounds lovely, Aunt Isabelle, thank you."

"Shall I expect Belle?"

"No, ma'am. Belle is going with her father and Sophie to look for houses. Sophie thought Belle should have some say since she'll be spending quite a bit of time with them."

"That's generous of Sophia, don't you think?"

"Very." The word stuck in her throat. What was the matter with her? She should be glad Belle and Sophie were hitting it off so well.

"Wes is coming, as well," her aunt said. "I don't think he was too keen on the idea, but I laid one of my famous guilt trips on him, and he finally said he'd be here."

Lara smiled. Isabelle had a real knack for wording things in such a way as to generate the maximum amount of shame. She and Wes had talked about it often, and while they both hated it when she turned the talent to them, it never failed to get results.

"Great," she said. "I haven't seen him since he got back from New Orleans."

"Excellent. I'll expect you about ten-thirty tomorrow."

The following morning dawned relatively cool for the end of June. Knowing that her aunt would be horrified if she wore shorts, Lara donned a loose-fitting

floral dress in hues of bright pink, peach and red and
left her chin-length hair loose around her face. She
drove to the Duncan estate, hoping the temperature
stayed reasonable. If it did, maybe her aunt would have
brunch served in the garden, a place that had never
failed to fascinate Lara as a child, or even now, for
that matter.

As Lara pulled into the circle drive, she saw that
Wes's white antique roadster was already parked beneath the portico of the flagstone house. Built at the
turn of the century, the nearly-five-thousand-square-
foot house resembled a structure more suited to En-
gland or the Scottish moors. To call it a showplace
would be depreciative.

Helen, the woman who had been Isabelle's cook for
as many years as Ruby Delaney had cleaned for her,
answered the doorbell's summons, her ample girth
banded by a pristine white apron worn over a black
dress. Isabelle was one for tradition. Helen pushed
open the ten-foot-tall pocket doors that led to the library, complete with twelve-foot ceilings, a fortune in
leather-bound books and the requisite library ladder.
Lara's aunt and brother were seated on the Victorian
rose-striped sofa, delicate Staffordshire cups and sau-
cers in hand.

As usual, Wes, who reminded her of Dylan Mc-
Dermott, looked as if he needed some care. His shirt
could have used a touch-up by an iron, and he looked
as if he hadn't shaved that morning. His hair, usually
too long because he got too involved in his painting
to take care of more mundane tasks, looked as if it had
received a recent cutting.

He smiled when he saw her and, ever the Southern
gentleman, got to his feet. A fleeting ache filled her

heart. Once their father died and Wes, who no longer felt the need to rebel against every command Phil Grayson had decreed, had put his wild ways behind him, he'd become a good man. But he was as luckless at finding a life partner as Lara had been.

"Miz Lara's here, Miz Isabelle," Helen said.

"Thank you, Helen," Isabelle said, as Wes gave Lara a hug and a quick peck on the cheek. "How far off is brunch?"

"Now why'd you ask me that?" Helen said, planting her fists on her substantial hips. "You know it's gonna be ready at eleven, just the way you asked, just the way I been doin' for all these years."

Helen slid the door shut and Lara and Wes exchanged quick, conspiratorial grins. The aging cook was the only person they knew who could talk back to their aunt and get away with it, a perk that came with their long association and had more to do with genuine friendship than an employer-employee relationship.

"That mouthy woman is going to get herself fired one of theses days," Isabelle grumbled.

"We've been hearing that since we were kids," Wes said. "You know you couldn't make it without Helen."

Isabelle smiled. "You're right. Unfortunately, Helen knows it, too."

"Speaking of brunch, is it too hot for us to have it outside?" Lara asked.

"Not for me," her aunt said. "There's a decent breeze this morning. I'll have Helen set the table out by the roses."

"Why don't I go ask her?" Wes said. "Since you

ticked her off, she might take the request better from
me. And I can move the table.''

''Everything ticks her off these days,'' Isabelle
grumbled. ''But by all means, be my guest.''

Wes winked at Lara and left the room, leaving behind the scent of something masculine and expensive.

''Pour yourself come coffee, Lara dear, and we'll
go have a look around while we wait.''

''That sounds lovely.'' Lara poured herself some
coffee from the silver pot and followed her aunt out
onto the terrace.

''Let's go look at the roses,'' Isabelle said. ''I want
to show you the statue Wes shipped me from New
Orleans. Heaven only knows what he paid for it.''

''You're not supposed to worry about that,'' Lara
said. ''You're just supposed to enjoy it.''

''I certainly will.''

The statue was a bronze angel almost five feet tall.
She was leaning over, with her wings outspread, as if
to protect whatever was beneath them.

''It's fantastic,'' Lara said, meaning every word.
''Wes has a true eye for the unusual, doesn't he?''

''He certainly does,'' Isabelle agreed.

Lara meandered down a path, crushing the chamo-
mile and thyme that grew between the cracks of the
flagstone. She breathed in their scent and felt at peace
for the first time since she'd awakened.

An ongoing project, Isabelle's garden would never
be complete. She was always finding a new piece to
add to one of her garden ''rooms'' as she called them,
moving others and trying new cultivars of her favorite
flowers.

Her most impressive contribution was her waterfall.
She'd made use of a natural hill, piped water to the

top, laid rock, dug a large pool and a stream that wound through the garden. She'd planted trees around the hill, along with a profusion of perennial ferns and a weeping willow. In spring and summer, iris and water hyacinth bloomed there, along with other plants that Lara had never seen before. Water ran continuously over what looked like a natural waterfall of moss-covered rocks, and meandered throughout the two-acre garden, composing an ever-changing melody that soothed even the most jangled nerves. At one point, where the flagstone path led to a gazebo—all but hidden by banana trees—a red-lacquered Japanese bridge crossed the stream.

It was truly a magical place, filled with expensive statuary garnered from Isabelle and Leo's travels, with more modern and less costly whimsical surprises, like the miniature bronze fairy that peeked out from behind a mossy rock and a collection of antique gates that supported various climbing vines. Filled with quiet places of contemplation, the tranquil setting was also a natural habitat for all sorts of birds, insects and forest creatures, something that might seem of secondary importance, but a fact that Lara knew was part of the reason behind the seeming randomness of the garden's design.

Donovan had helped create it.

As a teenager looking for work, he'd been the one who, at Isabelle's instruction, had stacked every rock and planted every tree for the waterfall. He was the one who'd mixed beer and moss together and spread it over the rocks to encourage more moss to grow. Now, after twenty years, it looked as if it had always been there.

"He has a knack, too, doesn't he?" Isabelle said.

"Who?"

"Donovan."

Something about the way Isabelle was looking at her made Lara uncomfortable. Again, she couldn't shake the feeling that her aunt knew more about her relationship with Donovan than she could.

"I couldn't really say," she said, aware that she sounded stuffy and stiff. "I haven't seen any of his work. As for all this, he did a good job of providing the muscle for your ideas."

"Actually, most of the waterfall and stream was his idea. He said he'd seen a waterfall in a magazine once and wanted to try to recreate it. When he suggested something I knew wouldn't work, I'd steer him straight, but this was pretty much his baby, as they say."

Lara was impressed. Donovan couldn't have been more than eighteen when he'd helped Isabelle with the project. That he had such a talent at that age was nothing short of extraordinary.

"I know about the two of you, you know," Isabelle said, jolting Lara from her thoughts.

Her startled gaze met her aunt's. "Know what?"

"That you two were interested in each other. I know that when he was arrested, it broke your heart and that's partly why you let your father railroad you into marrying Reed. Sophie's the reason Reed never loved you, and Donovan is the reason you could never fall in love with Reed."

"How could you possibly know that?" Lara asked in little more than a whisper. She was so stunned it never even occurred to her to deny Isabelle's claim. "No one knew but me and Donovan. And later, Dad."

"You had to tell him because you were pregnant, didn't you?" Isabelle probed.

Fearing her legs wouldn't hold her, Lara sat down heavily on a concrete bench. She raised her tortured eyes to her aunt's. "Who told you about that? Dad?"

"No one told me, sweet Lara," Isabelle said, reaching out and touching Lara's cheek with her fingertips. "I made an educated guess. I've made it a habit to be observant. I listen, and I watch. I saw things happening with you through the years, like your brother going out of his way to aggravate your father because he'd figured out that nothing he said or did would ever meet with Phil's approval anyway. I saw you falling in love with Donovan."

"How?"

"I watched the two of you together when you were here and when he was at your place." Her eyes held a tender reminiscent smile. "It was so gradual and such a beautiful thing to see. I could probably even tell you when things got…serious."

"Intimate, you mean?"

Isabelle nodded. "The winter of your senior year, wasn't it? Around Valentine's Day?"

Lara felt the blood drain from her head. Had it been so obvious then? She'd thought she was being careful. What had she done differently? "And how did you find out about…about the…baby?"

"I was never able to carry a baby to full term, but I had three miscarriages. I know morning sickness when I see it."

"You never said anything to Dad?" Lara questioned.

"Why should I? I could see that the two of you were good for each other, and I knew that if anything happened, Donovan would take care of you." She sat down next to Lara on the stone bench, as if the weight of her story was too much for her old legs to carry, and patted Lara's hand. "And then Hutch was killed, and there was no way Donovan could take care of you, was there?"

"No," Lara said with a shake of her head and tears burning in her eyes. She turned to face her aunt. "I don't know what to say."

"Why should you say anything?"

Lara's hand tightened around Isabelle's. "I wish I'd known you suspected something. I could have used a sounding board from time to time."

"You wouldn't have talked about it if I hadn't brought it up. I gave you an opening just yesterday, and you ignored it." Isabelle shook her head. "I knew I'd have to confront you head-on."

"Why didn't you ever mention it before now?"

"Back then I wasn't sure, and I knew better than to get between Phil and Rowland and their plans. And I thought that maybe things would work out between you and Reed. I've always been a romantic, and I thought you might turn to each other in your grief.

"I considered confronting you about it later, when it became clear that what you felt for each other was never going to turn into real love. Then you came up pregnant, and I didn't think I should rock the boat. I didn't know if you'd forgotten Donovan or not. And then, after you and Reed split up, you seemed happier, and I thought you might be ready to go out and find someone else."

"I've never forgotten Donovan."

"I know. I thought you might unburden yourself to me, but you're too much like your mother. She never once mentioned how miserable she was with your father, but I knew.''

"She didn't love him?"

"Oh, she loved him," Isabelle said in a dreamy, faraway voice. "She loved him too much. The problem was, your father liked other women. And the older he got, the younger he liked them. I think it had something to do with his knowing he was getting older. That macho thing."

Lara thought about that. She'd been very young when her mother died, and had few memories of what life had been like with her alive. She'd had no idea her dad had cheated on her mom, though as she got older, she knew he had a string of mistresses. He'd been discreet, though, and had never brought any of his women to the house. Lara had been smart enough to know it wasn't her place to question him about them.

She shook her head to rid it of thoughts of her father. None of that mattered now. What mattered was that Isabelle knew about Donovan, had always known.

"Why did you decide to tell me now?"

"Because Donovan has come back, and he would never have come back if it weren't for some good reason. Since Lewiston hasn't been particularly kind to the Delaneys, and it isn't a big city with lots of money, this isn't the most logical place to try to build the kind of business he wants to." Isabelle shrugged. "I figured something—or someone—else must have brought him back. And the only notion that made any kind of sense to me was that he'd come back for you."

Chapter Five

"Dear God," Wes observed from behind them. "You and Donovan Delaney?"

Lara glanced over her shoulder and saw the shock on her brother's face. She'd been so engrossed in her conversation with Isabelle she hadn't heard his footsteps on the flagstone.

"I knew you were pining for someone, but Donovan Delaney?" he said, moving around the bench and facing them.

Lara felt her face grow hot. "And what's wrong with him?" she demanded.

"Nothing. I always sort of admired the guy. He was friendly but macho—a man's man you know? He worked like a dog and had a reputation he didn't deserve, from what I saw. He liked to fight, but he never instigated one, and the girls went ga-ga over him. But I have a hard time imagining you with him."

Lara wanted to ask Wes how much he'd overheard but decided against it. "No harder than I'm having picturing you with Justine Sutton," she said, feeling the need to take the offensive.

Any pleasure Lara might have gotten from the gibe vanished along with the color from Wes's face. Normally she wasn't the kind of person who got her kicks from exchanging barbs, but Isabelle had thrown her a curve, and she hadn't recovered.

"Who told you about Justine?"

"Reed."

"I'll kill him," Wes snarled, turning and retracing his steps down the path.

Lara looked at her aunt, who seemed, for the first time in a long time, at a loss either for words or a plan of action. Lara leaped to her feet and ran after her brother, calling his name. He didn't stop. Finally she grabbed his arm and pulled on it with all her strength.

"Wes, please!" He turned and crossed his arms over his chest, but he wouldn't look at her. "I'm sorry," she said softly. "I had no idea you'd be so upset. All Reed said was that you asked Justine out when he asked out Sophie the first time."

He turned his head and met her gaze. The torment in his eyes was Lara's second shock of the morning. Her heart sank. Obviously, there was more to Wes and Justine's relationship than anyone suspected, and, in typical Wes Grayson fashion, he'd kept it to himself.

"That's all he said?"

"Yes."

He exhaled a harsh breath, shook his head and tipped it back to stare up at the canopy of leaves above them. Finally he gave a short, humorless laugh and found Lara's gaze once more. "So if I hadn't flown off the handle, that would have been the end of it?"

She nodded. "Probably so."

"I guess that's what happens when you have a temper with a hair trigger."

Obviously there had been more than one date. "Do you want to talk about it?"

Wes's gaze moved to the bench where Isabelle sat, watching them intently. "With you and Aunt Isabelle? Surely you jest. You know I don't talk about things like that."

"It might do you good. Maybe that's what's the matter with us Graysons. We keep too much inside. Maybe we should get it out."

"And maybe you should mind your own business."

"How much did you hear about me and Donovan?"

"That's about it."

"Aren't you curious?" she taunted, a hint of a smile on her lips. Maybe if she lightened things up a bit, he'd see things her way.

"Actually, I am, yes," Wes said, with a reluctant smile of his own.

"Quid pro quo?"

"You tell me something about you and Donovan, and I tell you something about me and Justine?"

"Yeah," she said, nodding. "No more secrets, Wes. And no more lies. At least not between us. From what I've learned since Sophie and Donovan came back here there have been enough lies and secrecy to last a lifetime."

Wes thought about it for a moment.

"I'm your sister, Wes. You know that anything you tell me will be kept in strictest confidence."

He sighed, nodding. "I know, and you're probably

right. But not today. Give me some time to get used to the idea of spilling my guts, which is something I usually reserve for my painting.''

True enough. Painting had always been a way for him to deal with his own emotions. It was the setting of his paintings, the use of color, the careful choice of details in everything from background objects to facial expressions to the clothing the people wore that combined to reveal the sentiment behind Wes's state of mind at the time the painting was executed.

Lara knew it was all she'd get that day, and coming from him, it was a lot. "Fair enough.''

Despite the encounter between her and Wes, the time spent with Isabelle was a success. As usual, Helen had outdone herself, and everyone had eaten far more than they should have. Wes left soon after the meal, claiming he was in the middle of the best painting he'd done in a long time.

"So, how is it going with the lovebirds?'' Isabelle asked.

"Sophie and Reed?'' Lara asked. "Well, things aren't perfect, but I think it's going to work out just fine. They're hoping to be married and settled by the time Cassidy starts school in August.''

"Sounds impossible to me.''

Lara smiled. "Well, they may not be settled. I certainly don't think Sophie will have the doors to her practice open by then. She hopes to have all her current patients settled in with someone else in Baton Rouge within the month and get herself and Cassidy moved soon after.''

Isabelle shook her head. "It's still a lot to get done.''

"I agree," Lara said. "But they're only having a small wedding. Immediate family and a few friends. Of course Celeste would like to have a lavish reception, but Rowland is being his usual obnoxious self, so I imagine Reed will nix that."

"What's Rowland up to?"

"The usual. Trying to put a wedge between Reed and Sophie by undermining her. He hasn't even met Cassidy yet, and she's his granddaughter."

Isabelle stopped short and looked at Lara with rampant disbelief shining in her eyes. "You're not serious?"

"Oh, but I am."

"That's terrible." Isabelle's eyes took on a thoughtful expression. "I don't know why Rowland is such a snob. Heaven knows his family wasn't much, so he shouldn't cast any stones at Sophie. He just happened to be very smart and able to bring himself up by the bootstraps, the same way she's done. The fact that he was handsome and charming as well as being an excellent doctor didn't hurt. Neither did his marrying Andrew Jefferson's only daughter." Isabelle gave another shake of her head. "She's a fool for putting up with all his infidelities."

"I agree," Lara said, "but I doubt she'd ever confront him about it. Not after so many years."

"You're probably right."

"Miss Isabelle! Are you out here?"

The masculine voice interrupted their conversation and brought Lara's head up like a doe scenting immediate danger. Donovan! Her heart began to pound and her questioning gaze found Isabelle's.

"We're out here by the roses, Donovan," she called back in a surprisingly strong voice. Then, to Lara, she said, "No, my dear, I didn't ask him to come today. I did, however, tell him to stop by one day when he was free, to see how the garden had grown since he'd been gone."

But he saw my car. He knew I was here. Why didn't he just keep driving? Why put us both through this torment? The thoughts scrambled through her mind, but all she said was, "Oh."

"If you're uncomfortable seeing him, you can go back to the house by the other path," Isabelle suggested, twin lines of worry drawing her perfectly drawn eyebrows together.

As it had since he'd come back, confusion took control of her. She felt like one of the teachers at school who was trying to quit smoking but carried around an unlit cigarette. Or an alcoholic in need of a drink from the unopened bottle sitting on the table before him. Though she wasn't certain she wanted her sharp-eyed aunt gauging every look and word that passed between herself and Donovan, Lara was reluctant to leave. She did and didn't want to be with him.

What she really wanted was to be with him without feeling either that searing pain or the devastating anger, but she wasn't sure that was possible. But there was at least a smidgin of a chance of that happening today, since neither of them was apt to let go with their true feelings as long as Isabelle was around.

Suddenly, Donovan rounded a curve in the path, which was blocked by some gigantic holly bush arch, and Lara's breath stopped. He was gorgeous in slacks and a blue, green and purple madras short-sleeved shirt that made his eyes look even bluer. In all the years she'd known him, Lara didn't recall seeing him in anything but jeans. As Aunt Isabelle was fond of saying, he cleaned up real nice.

"Hello, ladies," he said to them both with that slow smile of his.

Lara murmured a reply, and Isabelle echoed Lara's earlier thoughts. "My, don't you look nice."

"Thank you. It's Saturday, and I decided Jett and I needed some time off. I'm on my way to see the Doug Abernathy exhibit."

"I didn't know you were an art aficionado," Isabelle said.

"Yes, ma'am. I'm a particular fan of wildlife art. I don't know much about any of it, but I'm an amateur photographer, and I like what Abernathy does with light. I think I read somewhere that he was influenced by Monet." Donovan grinned. "Or was it Manet who painted that haystack in different degrees of light?"

"I always get them confused, too," Isabelle said with a chuckle.

"Manet," Lara said, speaking for the first time. Both pairs of eyes turned to her. "It was Manet who painted the haystack so many times."

"I believe you're right," Isabelle said.

Donovan plunged his hands into his pockets. "You look very pretty today, Lara," he observed, as if really seeing her for the first time. As if he hadn't been giving her sidelong glances ever since he arrived. "All cool and summerlike."

"Thank you," she said, though she didn't feel cool at all. She felt feverish. She knew her face was flushed and that her temperature must have risen at least a couple of degrees.

Donovan saved her from saying or doing something stupid by walking over and touching the blossom of a deep burgundy rose. "Is this the Don Juan we planted?"

"It certainly is. Gorgeous, isn't it?"

"It is that." Donovan grinned and held out his arm to Isabelle in an old-fashioned gesture. "Let's go see the waterfall."

"Your baby," she said, smiling up at him as she curved her fingers around his forearm.

He winked at her. "My baby." He turned to Lara and held out his other arm. "Ms. Hardisty?"

Knowing Isabelle was keenly interested in her response to Donovan, Lara wasted no time taking his proffered arm. She didn't want Isabelle thinking she was still pining for him. His tanned skin was warm to the touch, the flesh firm and the dark hair tantalizingly familiar beneath her fingertips.

His eyes met hers, and she knew he was remembering, too. Then, determinedly it seemed, he started down the path to the waterfall. When they reached the area where the pool spread out to the rock-edged gardens, he stopped, and Lara and Isabelle released his arms. No one spoke as he put his hands on his hips and studied the scene before him, no doubt remembering what it had looked like when first planted and thinking how far it had come.

"It's better than I dreamed it would be," he said finally. "More impressive than the pictures I've seen of it."

Lara knew the waterfall had been featured in a couple of magazines through the years. Isabelle never failed to give Donovan credit for the design and work, which, no doubt had helped him get where he was today.

"It looks as if it's always been there, doesn't it?" Isabelle asked.

He nodded. "That's the thing about a good plan. Sometimes when things are complicated, you have to put in a little more planning and effort to get it off the ground, but once everything is established, all you need is a little TLC to keep things in top shape."

As he spoke, he glanced over at her. Lara couldn't help feeling he was talking about something other than landscape design. Were his comments an allegory to them and their plans, plans that had seemed so good and plausible seventeen years ago? Was he alluding to the possibility that those plans might be salvaged? There was no clue to his thoughts revealed in his eyes. There was nothing there but a look of quiet satisfaction.

"Everything looks great, Isabelle," he said, sliding an arm around his mentor's shoulders. "But I knew it would." He pressed a kiss to her rouged cheek and gave her shoulders a light squeeze. "I can never thank you enough for all you've done for me."

A lump formed in Lara's throat. She knew he was talking about more than the knowledge Isabelle had imparted to him as a youth. He was talking about her relationship with his mother, which had gone beyond that of employer and employee. He was talking about her unfailing belief in him, the financial support that had paid for his attorney and her willingness to go the extra mile to see that he got a chance to start over in Lewiston. Lara knew there weren't many men secure enough in themselves to make such a comment in front of a third party. Neither her ex-husband nor her brother would have.

"It was my pleasure," Isabelle said, glowing from the sincerity of his gratitude.

Donovan looked at the no-nonsense watch strapped around his brawny wrist. "I'd better get a move on. I have a meeting before I go to the gallery. I don't suppose you ladies would like to go with me to see the art exhibit."

"Thank you, Donovan," Isabelle said, "but I'm about ready for my afternoon nap." She cast a sly glance at Lara. "Maybe Lara would like to join you. She's all alone, since Reed has Belle for the day."

It was all Lara could do to keep her mouth from falling open in surprise. Isabelle had the tact of a steamroller. "Oh, no, I couldn't," Lara said, a half smile jittering across her lips. "I have some…uh, reports I have to go over. You know summer school will be over in two weeks, and—"

"I understand," Donovan interrupted before she was forced into an outright lie. "Maybe another time."

She nodded weakly.

His eyes said he knew she lied, but he only smiled and pressed a kiss to Isabelle's rouged cheek. "Thanks for asking me to stop by. It was a pleasure, as usual."

"For me, too, and you're very welcome," she said. "I'll be calling you soon about a couple of ideas I have."

"Anytime." Donovan turned to Lara. "Goodbye, Lara."

"Goodbye." She watched him go, wishing with all her heart she'd had the courage to say she'd go with him. Wishing she could fully set aside her hurt and that they hadn't lost seventeen years….

Lara left Isabelle's soon after Donovan. The afternoon stretched out before her, long and lonely. Like

Donovan, Reed was taking Sophie, Cassidy and Belle to Little Rock to see the art exhibit. They would follow that with dinner and a movie, so it would be late when they got home. Reed had suggested that it made more sense for Belle to stay over than for Lara to wait up. Sophie and Cassidy would be staying at Donovan's while they were in town.

Again, Lara found herself wishing she'd gone with Donovan. She'd loved to have seen the exhibit. The wildlife artist was one of her favorites. She thought about calling Wes to see if he wanted to go with her and decided against it. Her brother had had about all the socializing a loner such as he could handle for one day.

As she changed into shorts, she wondered if Reed and Sophie had found a house. As far as Lara knew, there weren't too many nice ones available in Lewiston. Of course, they could always build. She wondered what it would be like to look for a place—a home— with the man you loved. Wondered what it would be like to spend time with someone whose very nearness made your palms sweat and your heart race.

Still, as happy as she knew Reed and Sophie were, she didn't envy them and their current situation. It must be miserable to want to be alone with the man you loved, wanting to make mad, passionate love and have two girls tagging along so that any intimacy was impossible.

Face it, Lara. You're jealous. Jealous of Reed and Sophie's happiness. Feeling sorry for yourself because it isn't you who's looking for a place and planning a wedding. You're going to wind up a lonely old woman

*if you don't snap out of it and start taking a more
active role in life.*

Easier said than done, unless she took Reed's advice, the same advice she'd given him at the Woodcutters' Festival. Which was what? To go after whatever it would take to make her happy? To throw
caution to the wind and follow her heart? Not to settle
for second best?

The problem was that first she had to decide just
what it would take to make her happy. Well, that was
a no-brainer. All it would take was Donovan Delaney.
Pure and simple.

*Would he really make you happy, or are you so
caught up in the beauty of Reed and Sophie's resur-
rected relationship that you're wishing you and Donovan could have the same thing?*

Maybe she was hoping that. There was nothing
wrong with having hopes and dreams, was there? Lara
knew they'd both changed, but other than becoming
more secure in who she was and finally finding some
backbone, she was still more or less the person he'd
claimed to love. Older. A few pounds heavier. But still
introverted and a bit shy, something she managed to
cover up beneath a cool and sometimes haughty de-
meanor. She still needed someone to give her a little
push every now and then to take a step out into the
vast ocean called life and to see what it had to offer.
Taking the passive approach was so easy when it came
to dealing with her personal life.

Donovan was the same as he had been, too. No,
definitely not. Impossible. No one could go through
the things he had and stay the same. But even though
he'd suffered hurt from his father and ridicule from the
townsfolk and God knows what in prison, none of it

had altered his basic personality. He still worked hard, still gave his best and, in spite of everything, he had a positive outlook on life. He had an innate self-confidence and wasn't afraid to rock the boat by trying something different. He didn't seem to be afraid of anything. And he was still a good person. As Isabelle often said, anyone could look good from time to time, but true goodness went bone deep.

Wes couldn't wait to leave his aunt's. He'd hardly been able to keep his mind centered on the conversation at lunch for thinking that his secret was out. He couldn't believe Reed had told Lara about Justine, but then, from what she'd said, he only mentioned it in passing. Of course Reed had known they'd seen each other more than once, and he had to have known the dates weren't innocent.

But Reed had no way of knowing that Wes had broken all three of his engagements at the last moment because he hadn't been able to get Justine Sutton out of his mind. Nor did Reed—or anyone—know that Wes had spent the night with Justine in Chicago almost five months ago and that he'd been like a man possessed ever since.

The few hours they'd spent together had shown him what he'd known for years: he might hate her for leaving town without so much as a phone call to tell him goodbye, but a part of him still cared for, still needed the down-to-earth solidity she'd brought into his life. Wes had needed that, back when he was seeing her. Needed it still. But she'd hurt him when she left without a word, and as much as he might long to pick up where they left off, he wasn't the kind of man to make the same mistake twice.

Oh, yeah? What about Chicago?

Chicago hadn't been anything meaningful. *Yeah, right.* It was just that they'd both had a little too much to drink at dinner, and they'd been discussing old times, and well, he wasn't proud of his brief lapse, but it had happened. Just because she'd spent the night in his bed didn't mean there were any deep and abiding feelings involved.

Then why can't you forget about it? Why did you leave Chicago and head straight for the Ford clinic, knowing it was time to do something about your drinking? And why haven't you been able to paint since then?

"I'm painting," he said, as if speaking the words aloud gave them more credence.

Yes, he was finally painting again, had been ever since he got back from New Orleans. He was working on a Mardi Gras ball scene set in the half-circle ballroom of Nottoway Plantation with lots of architectural detail and dozens of costumed guests. Unfortunately, the eyes behind every feminine mask were Justine's, as were the lips beneath every straight nose and the body of every woman in the room.

When he'd realized what he was doing, he decided to call the painting "Obsession." Even now he couldn't wait to get back to it, certain it was a piece that would never be for sale.

When Lara got home, she straightened up, watered her house plants and turned on the sprinkler in the front lawn. She did a couple of loads of laundry, made some slice-and-bake cookies and ate three of them with a cup of cappuccino. Then, at a loss as to what to do with the rest of her afternoon, she put on her swimsuit and swam a few laps. Exhausted for the moment, she stretched out on the lounger to get some sun while listening to Kenny G. When her skin began to tingle, she moved the lounge chair to the shade and started the newest Robert B. Parker book.

She loved the repartee between Spenser and Susan, but the very solidity of their closeness only made Lara more aware of just how long it had been since she'd been loved by a man and how lonely she was. At loose ends and still feeling guilty about the cookies, she set the book aside and dove back into the water.

It was nearing seven when, starving, she decided she'd had enough. She felt guilty for not using tanning lotion, but she was too hungry to hold off dinner until she could shower away the chlorine and slather herself in moisturizer to try to undo any potential sun damage. Instead, she picked up the rose-scented hand cream from the cabinet top, squeezed some into her palm and rubbed it over her shoulders and arms.

She surveyed the pantry's contents for something fast and decided she'd have some tuna salad, sliced tomato and cucumber and wheat crackers. Fast. Easy. Healthy. Then she'd take a nice cool shower and pray there was something on one of the almost fifty channels piped into her home by the local cable company.

She was pouring herself a glass of iced tea when the front doorbell rang. She frowned. Who on earth could be coming to visit at this time of evening on a Saturday? She padded barefoot to the door and looked through the peephole. It was a man, standing with his back facing her and his hands on his hips. She recognized the slacks and shirt and sucked in a startled breath.

Donovan!

Her first thought was that she wished she'd put on some clothes before she started her dinner. It was quickly followed by a question: What on earth was he doing there? He seemed to have a knack for showing up at the most inopportune times—and without any warning!

She didn't want to face him. Not while her defenses were so low. Not when she was feeling weepy and vulnerable and...needy. Maybe if she was very quiet and didn't answer, he'd go away.

Almost as soon as she'd had the thought, he turned and looked straight at the peephole, as if he could see her standing there, her eye trained on him.

"Open the door, Lara," he said. "I know you're in there, because your car is in the garage and there's music playing out back."

She chewed on her lower lip. Darn! Why hadn't she turned off the CD?

"I'm not leaving, so if you don't want the neighbors to wonder what I'm doing sitting on your front stoop a couple of hours from now, you'd better let me in."

He'd do it, too, she thought, her eyes narrowing in irritation. *The nerve of him!* Without stopping to think, she flipped the lock and jerked the door open. "What *are* you doing on my front stoop?" she asked, placing her hands on her hips in a mimicry of his stance.

He brushed past her into the foyer, carried along by his determination and a raw, pulsing energy that radiated from him in almost tangible waves.

"Sophie told me I should let you have your say. I should let you get it all out. Everything. How you felt when you heard about what I'd...about what happened. How you felt when I wouldn't see you. All of it. She says a festering wound won't heal. And I want it to. I need it to heal.''

Lara closed the door, so taken aback she couldn't think of a thing to say. Though she'd ached to tell him her feelings for seventeen long years, now that he was giving her the opportunity, her mind was as blank as a clean blackboard.

He paced to the end of the hallway, rubbing his forehead with his fingertips as he spoke. ''I canceled my meeting. When I left you and Isabelle, I went straight to the exhibit, and who should I meet but Reed, Sophie and the kids. It was like a slap in the face. They were all so damned happy, laughing and joking....''

He turned toward her, his face a study in sincerity and dismay. ''It hit me like a ton of bricks. I want what they have.'' He held up a fist, as if he were holding something inside. ''I had it in my hand, and I was robbed of it. I want it back, but I know I can't have it until we clear the air.''

Lara had never seen him so upset or so vocal about his feelings. ''What does our clearing the air have to do with your having what Reed and Sophie have?'' she asked, though on some level she knew where he was headed. Her heart beat out a sluggish, heavy rhythm.

He looked stunned by the question. For the first time he seemed aware that she was actually there. His gaze raked her from head to toe. Lara was uncomfortably aware that the black bathing suit she wore was cut high on the thigh and to the navel in front, the vee created by the two halves of the bodice held together by small lacing of scarlet. It was out of style, but she knew it looked good on her, so she kept it, even though she felt daring and half naked when she put it on. At that moment she felt naked in more ways than one. She wasn't prepared for this, for him. She didn't like being caught off guard.

"Because I want it with you," he said, but his gaze was focused on her body. "I told you that you were the reason I came back." He shook his head and gave a wave of his hand toward the stairs. "Go put on some clothes."

The simple command cut through her disorientation and nudged to life the anger usually kept under strict control. Who did he think he was, to come into her home and tell her how to dress! She crossed her arms over her breasts. "I'm fine."

"You're very…distracting."

"Get over it."

In a matter of seconds the nervous energy driving him as he'd pushed into the house dissipated like an early-morning mist beneath the rising sun. His shoulders slumped, and he raked a weary hand through his dark hair. The eyes that met hers were bleak with remorse and pain.

Lara hardened her heart to a reciprocal ache.

"God knows I've tried to get over it," he told her. "I can't. Every good memory I have is tied directly to you."

Like a bird of prey swooping down and snatching an unsuspecting creature from its hiding place, her hand shot out and connected smartly with his cheek.

His head jerked up in an involuntary reaction, and his eyes, wide with surprise, met hers. He lifted his hand and touched his cheek. "I guess I deserved that."

"You're darn right you deserved it, and lots more," she said in a voice quavering with anger. "How dare you muscle your way into my house and oh, so generously give me permission to tell you how I felt about the way you threw my love back in my face so *you* can feel better? You're the one who didn't believe in me—in us—enough to let me help you through one of the worst times of your life, so don't you dare stand there so pitiful and sad looking and expect me to feel sorry for any pain you may feel!''

"Lara." He reached for her, but she danced out of his grasp.

"There was a time I might have been impressed by your pretty little speech, but it's about seventeen years too late."

A spasm of pain crossed Donovan's rugged features. He plunged his hands into the pockets of his slacks. "I know I hurt you, but..." His explanation trailed away. "I don't know how to make you understand."

"Well, you wanted to talk about it, so try."

He nodded. "You were Lara Grayson. The banker's daughter. Richest girl in town, but somehow not spoiled by that. You were decent and caring, and somehow you came to care for me. You were everything good and decent in my life, and I was nobody. The local drunk's son who got charged with his murder. I didn't feel good enough for you before that happened, much less after I was charged. I knew there would be a lot of publicity, and—'' he brushed a weary hand over his forehead ''—it just all fell apart."

As he spoke, Lara's eyes filled with tears that ran down her cheeks. She swiped at them with trembling fingers. "I loved you!" she said in a soft, urgent voice. "You were my best friend and my only lover. They said you were guilty of a terrible crime and hauled you off to jail. How could I not be touched by that? I *hurt* for you. I wanted to be there for you, and you cut me out of your life as if I was a deadly cancer.''

"Damn it, Lara, I did it for you! I didn't want you to be dirtied or hurt by it all, but it almost killed me.'' The last few words were ground out through gritted teeth.

Like all men, he was unmovable. "You should have let me have a say in whether or not I wanted to be dirtied by it. After everything you claimed I meant to you, you owed me that much.''

She thought she saw the glitter of tears in his eyes.

"You meant everything to me, and I owed you a lot more than that,'' he told her. "I owed you everything I was, everything I ever hoped to be. I still do.''

"Then you owe me the truth about what really happened.''

He grew very still. A wary expression entered his eyes. "What do you mean? You know the truth.''

"Yes,'' she said, nodding, "I do. But not because you trusted me enough to tell me. Reed did.''

"What did Reed tell you?''

"That Sophie shot your father, not you. That she was pregnant with Cassidy, and you knew she couldn't take going to jail, so you took the fall for her.''

Donovan closed his eyes, and reached up to pinch the bridge of his nose as if to ease a pain centered there. "I can't believe he told you. He wasn't supposed to say anything.''

"He told me about Sophie confessing to the sheriff and that Micah said to let it be. Reed didn't think Sophie would mind, and he thought I needed to know the truth.''

"Why now?''

She shrugged. "Well, evidently he just learned the

truth himself, and he told me because he saw us by the pool the other night and finally figured out that you were the person I was trying to get over when I married him.''

"Why did you marry him?" Donovan asked. "I know now that Rowland used marriage to you as a tactic to divert Reed's attention away from Sophie. I always supposed that you did it out of spite or revenge." He shook his head. "But I could never quite believe that. It didn't seem like your style."

It was the opportunity she'd waited for. Dreamed of. Rehearsed in her mind a million times. For a brief, panicked moment she wondered if she had the courage to say the words, wondered what his knowing would do to the feelings he claimed to still have for her. She decided it didn't matter. Just as Reed had deserved to know the truth about Cassidy, Donovan deserved to know the truth about the child she'd lost. Maybe then he'd understand why his actions had hurt so badly.

"Truth, Donovan?" she asked in a scornful voice.

"Of course I want the truth."

"You're right. I didn't marry Reed to get back at you, I married him because I was desperate."

"Desperate?"

"Yes, desperate! I had something important to tell you, and you wouldn't see me, wouldn't return my calls and sent my letters back unopened. I was pregnant, Donovan. While you were being noble and trying to save me, I was dying inside because I was carrying your baby, and I didn't know what to do about it.''

Chapter Six

Lara pregnant with his baby? Donovan knew his mouth had fallen open in surprise. He felt his legs go weak and a curious buzzing filled his brain. As unmanly as it might be, he had the sudden feeling he was going to faint.

"I need to sit down," he said. He didn't wait for her permission but turned and headed toward the living room. Lara followed. He sank into a generously designed armchair covered in a butter-yellow, royal-blue and fern-green stripe, propped his elbows on his knees and buried his face in his hands. Lara sat on the edge of the floral-patterned sofa done in the same bright colors.

After several seconds he lifted his head to look at her. "You aren't...just telling me this?"

The look that entered her eyes was deadly.

"Scratch that," he said with a shake of his head. "I

know you'd never lie about something like that, but I just don't understand how it happened.''

Lara's laugh was short and unpleasant. "You knew how very well, as I recall. I was the inexperienced one.''

"But I always used protection.''

She shook her head. "The world is full of babies whose parents used protection.''

Donovan scrubbed a hand over his face. A baby. He and Lara had made a baby together, and he hadn't known. No wonder she'd been so hurt when he refused to have any contact with her. Remembering how shy and introverted she'd been back then, just forcing herself to come to the jail must have been a major hurdle. But she had come, battling her timidity while trying to cope with what must have been extreme panic. And she'd been brave enough to do it knowing she was flaunting their relationship for the whole world and her family to see, and he—in his desire to do the honorable thing—had turned her away. He felt like crying for what he'd unknowingly thrown away, yet a part of him still believed he had done the right thing, the only thing he could have done under the circumstances.

He and Lara. A baby. The surprise of it gave way to a feeling of wonder. No wonder he felt such a kinship with Belle. The tenderness of his thoughts came to an abrupt halt. Lara had married Reed to give their baby a name, but Belle was too young to be that child. Donovan's questioning gaze found Lara's.

She looked back at him steadily. "I miscarried.''

The blunt, unadorned statement poleaxed him. For a moment he felt as if the breath had been knocked from him, and then the pain filled his mind and began to spread…all the way to the deepest hollows of his heart and the most sacred places in his soul.

Lara got to her feet and began to pace, as if the telling had released some sort of nervous energy. "Reed and I were only married three weeks when it happened. We'd just moved to Fayetteville and got settled in our apartment. We were both alone for the first time in our lives."

"No one came to help out?"

She offered him another of those bitter laughs. "Who? My dad the cool, calculated banker, or Reed's—the compassionate physician?"

"I thought that maybe Reed's mother…"

"I wouldn't let him call Celeste. He took me to the hospital, and when I came home, we managed." She sucked in an unsteady breath and sank back down onto the sofa. "He was wonderful, actually. As scared as he was, he did everything he could. Everything he knew how to—not that anyone could have offered me the comfort I needed at the time."

Donovan closed his eyes and tried to imagine Reed and Lara at eighteen and twenty years old, alone in a strange place, dealing with one of the most traumatic incidents in a person's life.

Lara propped her elbow on the sofa's padded arm and rested her chin on it. She gave him a sad little smile. "I suppose it's one of life's little ironies that if I'd waited awhile, I wouldn't have had to marry anyone. And maybe if Reed and I hadn't married, we could have both found someone. Maybe we could have been…happier."

Donovan could see that the unnecessary marriage weighed heavily on her mind. Somehow she blamed it for all her and Reed's unhappiness. Donovan tried to push aside his own shock and pain to help her find a way to rid herself of hers.

"How did your dad find out?"

"The man at the jail told him I'd been coming by and calling. Dad was smart. It didn't take him long to put two and two together and come up with three. He confronted me, so I had to tell him."

"Whose idea was it for you to marry Reed?"

"It was a mutual thing between my dad and his. They'd always hoped we'd marry, and they got their hopes up when we dated that short time." Her lips quirked briefly. "Remember how I told you that if I was dating Reed, no one would suspect there was anyone else? Well, that came in handy when I came up pregnant. The idea was that everyone would think it was Reed's baby when I began to show."

"You didn't tell anyone I was the father?"

"No," she said. "That I wouldn't be forced to tell was my one condition to the marriage." She let her head fall back against the cushions and looked up at the ceiling. "Dear God, what a mistake! It was a hard way to learn that two wrongs don't make a right. And I promise that if Belle ever gets in trouble I won't make her marry the guy unless it's something they both really want to do."

"Don't forget that if you hadn't married Reed, you wouldn't have Belle."

This time Lara's smile was bittersweet. "I know. It's another of those little ironies. She's the absolute very best of me and Reed."

"She's a great kid," Donovan said, nodding. "I'm crazy about her." He realized as he said the words that they were true.

"The feeling is mutual. Even after so little time with you, she thinks you hung the moon."

Neither spoke for several seconds. Finally Donovan ran a trembling hand through his short dark hair. "This wasn't as bad as I expected."

"No?" she queried. "What did you expect?"

"I don't know. Lots of yelling. Tears. Accusations."

"Me, too," she said with a nod. "I was looking forward to letting you have it."

"What happened?" he asked with a weak smile.

She shrugged. "Maybe I cried all my tears out a long time ago. Lord knows I've cursed you to hell and back a hundred times. When I thought about this moment, I always imagined you saying something and me just…snapping and letting you have it. Maybe you disarmed me by giving me permission to let it all out."

"I'm sorry," he said.

"For what? Disarming me or for what happened?"

"Both. But I'm especially sorry that you lost our baby." Even talking about it with her, it seemed unreal. He wished there were some part of himself and Lara as proof of their brief happiness. Wished he had a son or daughter to fight with over the choices and decisions he'd made. Wished he had someone to love him unconditionally. Of course, Sophie and Cassidy did, but it wasn't the same.

"I wish I had Reed's problem. I know Reed and Cassidy aren't having an especially easy time of it right now," he said in a voice choked with emotion. "But they'll work through it, and then they'll be glad they found each other."

Donovan saw Lara's eyes fill with the tears she thought she'd cried away. One slipped down her cheek, quickly followed by another and then another. With a little cry of dismay and maybe a little embarrassment, she buried her face in her hands.

The tears were his undoing. He was out of his chair in a second, crossing the few feet that separated them and going to his knees in front of her. He curled his fingers around her wrists.

"Lara." He pulled her hands away so that she had no choice but to look at him. The tears magnified the pain in her dark eyes.

"I'm sorry," he said, his voice urgent and low, thick with the emotion he tried so hard to hold back, even as he felt the sting of tears beneath his eyelids. "I loved you. I never stopped. I never meant to abandon you or to hurt you. I believed the decision I made would cause you the least harm. I swear it."

"I know." The two words were breathed out on a soft expulsion of air.

The hushed acknowledgment and the expression in her eyes that said he was forgiven was all it took to break the restraint holding back his own sorrow. "It hurts," he said, unable to stop the tears or a single harsh sob.

She slid her hands from his loose grasp and took his fingers in a tight grip. "I know."

And then, somehow, she was on her knees facing him, their arms locked tightly around each other, cheeks pressed close, their tears mingling. Her soft sobs tore at his already-bleeding heart, making him feel powerless and ineffectual, emotions he hadn't felt since he'd heard heavy metal prison doors clanging shut behind him.

His hands moved over her back in a gesture designed to comfort and found his own comfort in the familiarity of her. He felt her lips against his cheek, heard her heart-broken whisper in his ear.

"Don't cry. Please, don't cry." Anguish filled, the words—the same ones his mother had chanted to him as a child—brought back the pain of her death and a fresh round of tears. Tears of sorrow. Of regret. And release. Tears that cleansed the last of the bad feelings and old resentments away.

He wasn't sure how long they cried, but it seemed like half of forever. He felt as wrung out as if he'd just worked ten hours in the broiling sun, but when he was all cried out, his heart felt lighter, lifted of a load he'd carried for too many long and lonely years.

Relieved of that burden, the world around him made a gradual return. He heard the sound of children yelling down the street outside and the angry fussing of a blue jay. The ticking of the grandfather clock in the foyer. Lara's soft breathing. Her occasional sniff.

They were still holding each other. He felt the heat of her body pressed against him from knee to chest— two perfectly fitted puzzle pieces—and breathed in the scent of roses, not unlike the old-fashioned perfume his mother had worn when she dressed up and went to town. But unlike his mother's signature scent, which always made him feel safe and cared for, Lara's invoked an entirely different image.

Donovan had never considered himself fanciful, but the picture was as vivid as any landscape design to fill his mind. He saw her in a long-sleeved gown that covered her from the floor to the neck, all the more sexy because of its utter femininity and because the tiny pin tucks and delicate fabric hid—but suggested—the curves beneath, a subtle invitation to rip it off and expose what lay beneath. Dangerous thoughts. He drew in a shaky breath and forced his eyes open to banish the vision.

Her head lay on his shoulder, and her eyes were closed. He felt her breasts pressed against his chest and became aware that her fingertips were rubbing tiny circles on his back just above the waistband of his slacks. His own hands were at her waist, firm beneath the stretchy fabric of her swimsuit. Without thinking of the consequences, half expecting her to jerk free and throw another of those prissy "how dare yous" at him, he turned his head and pressed a featherlight kiss to the side of her neck.

Instead of retaliating, she grew still in his embrace, as if she were waiting to see what he'd do next. What he did was kiss her neck again, whisper-soft butterfly kisses, his lips barely grazing the fragrant flesh. When she still made no response, he grew bolder, adding the tip of his tongue to his enticement and moving his hands to her naked back, bared by the suit to the hollow just above the sweetly rounded curve of her bottom.

She dragged in a sharp little breath, and the tension holding her body intensified for heart-stopping seconds before draining away and leaving her body limp and malleable in his embrace. Emboldened, he allowed his lips to move up toward the curve of her jaw, trailing moist, openmouthed kisses along the path to his goal: her lips.

She must have known what he was about, because that fine, tangible tension returned. Fearing sudden and complete rejection, but desperate to taste her mouth again, he kissed her. Found her lips parted and receptive. He meant for it to be a little kiss, but the moment his mouth touched hers, reason fled before a flurry of sweet remembrances.

He wasn't a monk, but life had taught him the importance of control, and he didn't sleep around indiscriminately. Women in his life had been few and far between. None of them had ever made him feel what Lara did.

The way their mouths fitted together so perfectly hadn't changed. Neither had the taste of her. Honey. Ambrosia. Warm, willing woman. She still made those faint little sounds in her throat—sounds he'd filed away in his memory so he could take them out and relive them during the really bad times. Little soft sounds, something between a groan and a whimper.

He realized with something of a start that she'd slipped her hands into the back pockets of his slacks, urging him nearer, pressing against him and molding her curves to his body with a surprising and hungry impatience. He felt her tugging at his shirt, felt her hands slip beneath the fabric, seeking the heat of his flesh as if she needed to touch him as much as he needed her to.

Ah, Lara. Lara. Lara.

Her name throbbed through his mind in time with the blood pounding hotly in his head and in his veins, offering him a long-needed and often-longed-for solace. He moved his hands up to cradle her face gently, almost reverently, but bruising her mouth with hot, wet kisses that underscored his need and bordered on desperation. As needy as he, Lara gave him back kiss for kiss. Teeth nipped. Tongues darted, swirled, mated, a poor substitution for the real thing.

One hand moved up to touch her breast. She didn't stop him. Encouraged, he eased his hands down and insinuated his fingers beneath the straps of her bathing suit. Still meeting no resistance, he slipped the straps from her shoulder.

"Wait." A soft supplication.

He looked at her, and she smiled—part shyness, part coquette. Her fingers worked at the buttons of his shirt, freeing them from their moorings with quick efficiency, sliding her hands inside to touch his waist, bringing them around to his stomach and letting them drift upward.

With her fingers curled in the hair on his chest, she leaned forward and buried her face against him, her mouth moving over him, her breath tickling, her tongue tracing random patterns against his sensitive flesh.

Air trickled from Donovan's lungs in a slow hiss. Thinking was an impossibility. Capable of nothing but feeling and reaction, he captured her face once more and took her lips in another hungry kiss. She opened her mouth for the invasion of his tongue and slipped her hands up to ease the shirt from his shoulders.

He pulled his arms free. The shirt fell to the floor. He was aware of her moving, doing something, but as he was bent on plundering all the secret places of her mouth and functioning on pure desire, that something barely registered.

A brief flash of sanity warned him that if she didn't want this to happen, she would have to stop him soon. He felt her arms slide up around his neck, felt her surge against him and the warmth of bare flesh. Surprise ended the kiss and left him still, motionless. He drew back to look at her, the expression in his eyes asking her if she really wanted this to happen.

"Don't stop," she whispered. "Please, don't stop."

It was all the encouragement he needed.

Clothes were discarded with surprising efficiency and careless abandon. Hands and mouths explored, reacquainting themselves with peaks and valleys, gentle swells and caverns. Kiss was exchanged for sweet, hot kiss. Breath for breath. Blood raced. Pulses throbbed. Heartbeats pounded in perfect synchronization while desire rose in a heady, steady spiral.

He buried himself in her with a soft growl of pleasure. Intense. Almost painful. Hearing her reciprocal cry of gratification made him want it to last and last, but it had been so long…too long. And Lara was urging him to hurry…hurry…. Drowning in a sea of pure pleasure, he swallowed her cry of fulfillment and knew that at last he had come home.

They lay together on the sofa like two spoons in a drawer, Donovan's back to the sofa's; Lara's back to his front. Idly she rubbed her fingertips against the hair on the forearm that lay across her middle. Just as idly she wondered when and how they had gotten there and realized that it didn't matter. Nothing mattered except that she was back in Donovan's arms…where she belonged. Where she'd always belonged. She felt his lips against her shoulder. In spite of a lethargic weariness, she felt a little ripple of pleasure.

"What are you thinking about?" His voice was a low rumble in her ear, his breath warm.

"Nothing much," she answered.

"Regrets?"

Regrets? How could there be regrets when she was still having trouble putting two coherent thoughts together? Any regrets she might feel would have to come later. At the moment she would have to describe her feelings as complete contentment. Somehow in the narrow space allotted her, she managed to turn toward him. Her smile was as soft as the finger that smoothed his mustache.

"No," she assured him. "No regrets. You?"

"How could I have any regrets when this is what I've dreamed about for almost half my lifetime? I love you, Lara. I've never stopped loving you."

For long moments there was no sound in the room but soft moans and the ticking of the clock in the hall. Finally, with an effort, Donovan dragged his mouth from hers. "What time is it?"

She unwedged her arm from between them and looked at the marcasite watch circling her wrist. "Almost eight-thirty."

"What time does Belle get home?"

"She's staying over at Reed's."

Donovan's smile was soft and slow and incredibly sexy. He touched his forehead and nose to hers. "Good," he said on a sigh. "I'd really like a repeat performance."

It was almost midnight before Lara and Donovan finally succumbed to sleep, almost ten past when the man in the nondescript sedan, who was on his way home from an assignation himself, spotted the Explorer in Lara's driveway.

Kinda late for the principal to be entertaining, he thought, pulling to a stop near the curb. He wondered who the vehicle belonged to, mentally ran a check on the people in town he knew who owned that color, year and model. Through the process of elimination, he came up with the name Donovan Delaney.

Donovan Delaney and Lara Hardisty? The man

shook his head and rubbed his chin, a crooked smile on his face. Very interesting. He eased his foot off the brake, and rolled down the street. If word got out, it would be more grist for the town's gossip mill and apt to start quite a stir.

Donovan woke as the world was about to turn early-morning gray. He lay on his back with his arm flung up, his forearm over his face, and the moment he opened his eyes he realized he wasn't in his own bed. Remembrance washed over him. Lara. He turned his head and saw that she lay close to him, her hands tucked beneath one cheek, more beautiful in sleep than any woman ought to be. Careful not to wake her, he turned a bit and, leaning over, touched his lips to her forehead in the softest of kisses.

He longed to pull her close and hold her, but he knew that if he did, he'd be even later getting away. The thought of leaving her was a painful lump in his chest. Life had taught him that life was uncertain, and finding true happiness again, he was fearful that if he left, he'd lose it again.

But he wasn't a callow youth anymore, and Lara wasn't a careless teenager. They were adults with responsibilities. She held a high position in town. It wouldn't do for one of her neighbors to wake up, go out to get the morning paper and see him leaving in the wee hours. Staying as long as he had was more risk than he should have taken with her reputation.

With a sigh he swung his feet to the floor, found his clothes and pulled them on. He didn't like this sneaking-around stuff. As the current saying went, he'd been there, done that. Before, Lara had wanted to tell the world they were seeing each other. He'd been the one who'd hesitated. No more. This time he wanted to be up-front with the whole world. No more clandestine meetings. No more secret sex at her dad's lake cabin. No more sneaking around like thieves.

He'd paid his debt to society and was a tax-paying citizen of Lewiston. A business owner. A responsible member of society. He and Lara would talk, decide how to tell Belle, and announce the news to their families. Then he'd have her put news of their upcoming nuptials in the *Lewiston Gazette* and tell the whole world.

It was just daylight when Donovan turned the key in the lock and eased the door open, praying he wouldn't wake his sister or his niece. He felt as guilty as a teenager who'd stayed out past curfew. He didn't feel like explaining where he'd been, and he certainly didn't want to tell them what he'd been doing. It was best to just pretend he got in late. If Sophie even suspected he'd been with Lara, she would want to know every detail—not just what they'd done, but how he'd felt, how she acted, where he thought it was leading.

He didn't want to share his feelings just yet. It was too soon. Right now he just wanted to hold close the memories of the night, to guard them from prying eyes and savor them at his leisure. He slipped out of his shoes and, as quietly as possible, put on the coffee. It would be brewed by the time he finished his shower.

The water was hot, just the way he liked it. He lathered his body, thinking that he hated to wash away the sweet-smelling scent of roses that seemed to permeate every pore of his skin, a lingering reminder of what he and Lara shared. He toweled off, put on clean, faded jeans and a T-shirt and padded barefoot back to the kitchen.

The coffee was done, so he poured himself a mug full and took two packages of chocolate cream-filled cupcakes from the pantry. Taking a paper plate from the cabinet, he sat down at the table and ripped open the first package, trying to focus on what he needed to accomplish that day and realizing that he couldn't get past the need to talk to Lara.

At least wait until afternoon to call. Try to play a little hard to get.

It was good advice, he thought, taking a healthy bite of the first cupcake, even if it was like closing the gate after all the cows got out. He'd already told her he loved her, had never stopped, so what would waiting to call accomplish? Still, she'd probably sleep until late. He washed down the sweet with a mouthful of coffee.

He tried to ignore the tiny voice inside him that said there was more to his reluctance to call than he was willing to admit. He didn't want to contemplate the possibility that having time to think about what had happened might put a damper on Lara's emotions. She'd never been impulsive, and given an opportunity to think her actions through might make her more cautious than he'd like.

Forget it. Forget her.

Also good advice, since there was plenty to do besides mooning around like a lovesick kid. Donovan polished off the first cupcake and picked up the second, his mind made up. No matter how much he wanted to, he wouldn't call Lara until after lunch.

"Good morning." The husky words preceded Sophie into the room. Her strawberry-blond hair was tousled, and her blue eyes were drowsy with sleep.

"Morning." Donovan rose to give her a hug and guided her to a chair. "Sit," he urged, pushing her down gently. "I'll get your coffee."

She smiled, shoved a hand through her hair and propped her elbow on the table. "Thanks." She rested her chin in her palm.

"Did you have a good flight?"

"It was great," Sophie said with a sigh. "But I'm exhausted. I know Cassidy is, too."

"She'll probably sleep till noon."

"If Belle will let her."

"Belle? Did she sleep over?"

Sophie shook her head. "Believe it or not, Cassidy stayed at Reed's."

"Things must be going pretty well between the two of them, then."

"I think so." Sophie stirred a spoonful of sugar into her coffee. "You must have gotten in really late last night. I didn't get home until a little after eleven."

"Yeah." Donovan refused to offer her anything but the bare bones, which, when he saw the speculative gleam in his sister's eyes, he realized was a mistake.

"Ah," she said, a small smile toying with the corners of her mouth. "A woman."

He set the mug of coffee on the table with a thud. "What makes you say that?"

"Even if Lewiston wasn't dry, I can't see you hanging out at the local bar or the bowling alley, so it must be a woman."

Trying for nonchalance, he refilled his own coffee mug, sat down and began to unwrap the second pack of snack cakes. "I thought you were a shrink, not a detective."

Her eyes narrowed. "I'm a psychologist, not a shrink, and does that mean I'm right?"

"You're so darn smart," he said, picking up his coffee. "You tell me."

Holding her mug in both hands and with her lips still resting against the rim, Sophie inhaled a draft of the fragrant brew. She took a slow sip and regarded him with an unnerving steadiness. "Hmm," she said, setting down the coffee. "Unwarranted anger and—"

"I am not angry," he snapped, slamming down his own coffee mug so hard the liquid sloshed over the rim.

"—very defensive," she finished. She smiled sweetly at him. "Yep. It was a woman. Lara, I presume."

Donovan started to scoop up what was left of his breakfast and head for the door and thought better of it. What was the use denying the truth, especially since he wanted the whole world to know? Besides, Sophie wouldn't say anything until he gave her the okay.

"Yeah, it was Lara," he said, meeting her gaze with blatant defiance. "And yes, I stayed the night. Do you have a problem with that?"

Eyes wide, Sophie held her hands up, palms out. "Nope," she said, with a shake of her head. "No problem here. But I do have one thing to say."

"Yeah?" he growled. "What's that?"

"Hallelujah!"

Cassidy, who'd been awakened by Belle, was in the kitchen with her sister, looking through the contents of Reed's refrigerator and wishing she were sleeping when a knock—almost a pounding—sounded at the door.

Belle pulled a face. "Great," she said. "It's Grandpa Hardisty. I recognize his knock."

Cassidy felt her heart go into free fall while Belle went to unlock the door. Grandpa Hardisty. Reed's dad. Belle's grandfather and hers, too. Cassidy hadn't met Rowland Hardisty yet, but she knew enough about his part in her parents' pasts to know she didn't think she would like him much. Struck with a sudden panic, her gaze darted around the room, as if she hoped to find a way of escape and seeing nothing but the tumble of sheets on the sofa bed where she and Belle had slept. With nowhere to go, she moved behind the bar, all that separated the minuscule kitchen from the living room.

Feeling somewhat safer, she watched as Belle opened the door and a sixty-something man strode in. She was surprised to see that her grandfather was tall and slender, handsome, even. He looked the way she imagined her own father looking as he got older. Somehow, she'd expected Rowland to be big and blustery. Instead, he was sophisticated, polished and exuded an undeniable coldness. Maybe, she thought, suppressing the inadvisable urge to giggle, it was from spending so many hours in an operating room.

At first Rowland was so busy talking to Belle he didn't see Cassidy. When he did, he paused just inside the door. Cassidy felt the full impact of his piercing gaze.

"Who's your friend?" he asked Belle with a smile.

Though he pretended ignorance, Cassidy knew he must know exactly who she was.

"Oh," Belle said with a wide smile of her own and

a wave toward Cassidy. "This is Cassidy. She's your granddaughter, too."

Cassidy wanted to crawl in a hole. Surely there was some other way to break the news to him without being so blunt and insensitive. Rowland Hardisty looked as if he'd like to bite off someone's head. Belle looked extremely pleased with herself. Of course she would, Cassidy thought. Belle was nothing if not direct, and Cassidy was quickly learning that her little sister liked to stir the embers of controversy.

"So you're Cassidy?" Rowland asked, crossing the small room and extending his hand and a smooth smile. Cassidy had to give him points for recovering so quickly.

"Yes, sir." She reached across the Formica-topped bar and felt her hand taken in his. Surprisingly, his grip was firm and warm.

He released her hand and she breathed easier. Maybe this wouldn't be so bad. Maybe he'd be civil in front of Belle, even though Cassidy saw his dislike of her in his eyes.

"Where's your mother?"

The question caught Cassidy off guard. "She's staying at my uncle Donovan's place."

"Really? That surprises me. But then the Delaneys have always surprised me."

On the surface the comments seemed perfectly innocent, but Cassidy recognized it as the dig against her family that it was. At that moment she was certain she hated Rowland Hardisty. Why did he think he was so much better than her mom? So he was a doctor— a surgeon. Big deal. Maybe no one had bothered to tell him that her mother had a doctorate in psychology and that it took more than a fat bank account to be a decent person.

"Really? How's that?" she asked, forcing herself to meet the mockery in his eyes. Refusing to let him intimidate her.

"Well, for starters, I couldn't believe your uncle had the guts to come back here after what happened."

"Why would you think Sophie would stay here?" Belle asked, focusing on her grandfather's earlier statement. "She and Daddy aren't married yet."

"Good point, Belle."

Everyone turned toward the sound of Reed's voice. He stood in the doorway that led from the kitchen to his bedroom, wearing nothing but a pair of shorts.

There was an apology in his eyes, but there was steel in his voice as he said, "I can't imagine why Grandpa would expect to find her here, can you?"

"Nope."

Reed shook his head and crossed his arms over his bare chest. "Did you come for some specific reason, Dad? If so, spit it out. I'm taking my girls to breakfast before we pick up Sophie and go house hunting, and we really need to step on it if we're going to be on time."

Anger smoldered in Rowland Hardisty's eyes. "It was nothing important," he said, turning toward the door. "You might give me a call sometime when you aren't so busy."

"I'll do that," Reed said. He started toward the door. "Let me see you out."

Rowland had no choice but to follow. Cassidy watched as Reed ushered his father to the door. She heard his low "How dare you come into my house and pick on a sixteen-year-old kid" before the slamming door shut out everything except the indisputable sound of muffled, angry voices.

"Don't pay any attention to Grandpa," Belle said, coming to give Cassidy a hug. "He thinks he's so perfect."

"He never liked my mom, and he doesn't like me," Cassidy said, feeling the burning of tears in her eyes and smarting beneath the unfairness of it all. "And now I've caused Reed to fight with him."

"Believe me, that isn't your fault," Belle assured her. "They fight every time they're together. And as far as him not liking you and your mom, Aunt Isabelle says he doesn't even like himself."

"He doesn't even know me!" Cassidy said. "Or her, either."

"He'll come around," Belle said, offering her the advice she'd heard so often from her parents.

Cassidy couldn't doubt the sincerity in Belle's eyes, but somehow it didn't make her feel any better.

Chapter Seven

Lara awoke with a smile on her face. She felt vibrantly alive, pleasantly content and incredibly sexy. The scent of Donovan's cologne wafted up from the sheets. Just thinking about him made the smile grow wider. She was luxuriating in some pretty erotic memories when the phone rang.

She hated to answer, but a glance at the caller ID told her it was her aunt, and Lara was afraid something might be wrong. As it turned out, Isabelle just wanted to tell her that, due to some family emergencies, the school board meeting had been rescheduled for two weeks from Monday.

The small reminder pierced the bubble of Lara's happiness and brought her back to reality with sickening speed. The board would be making its yearly review of her work, so the meeting was an important one. Her contentment and joy made a sudden transition to concern. Had any of her neighbors seen Donovan's vehicle in the driveway all night? If so, had they recognized it? He'd left before daybreak, but old Mrs. Carruthers got up before dawn to get her paper. Had she seen the car? Or worse, had she seen Donovan leaving?

Lara showered, washing his scent from her body but unable to wash away her worry, which grew by the moment, especially when she tried to remember if Donovan had used birth control. She didn't think he had. Not the first time, anyway. But he'd always been so careful in the past. Maybe she just wasn't aware of it.

As if there wasn't enough on her mind, when Reed dropped off Belle just after lunch, a whole new worry rose to haunt her. She knew Donovan thought that what had happened between them was the first step to their becoming an item and ultimately a family. How would her daughter take to the idea of her mom seriously dating someone? Possibly marrying someone? Donovan Delaney to be exact. Belle liked him, almost worshipped him, in fact. But being his sidekick for a few hours at a time was far different from having him for a stepdad and living under the same roof.

Just as she and Reed did, Donovan would have likes, dislikes and rules, things that would upset the status quo. Belle was fairly easygoing, but she was already being blended into one new family, complete with a new sibling to learn to deal with and Sophie's rules. And much as Belle liked Sophie and Cassidy, the road wouldn't always be smooth. There would be times Belle would butt heads with the members of her new family. Was it fair to ask her to take on yet another change at this point in her life?

Lara fretted all day, wondering how she could relay her worries to Donovan without alienating him. She didn't want to lose him, but she wasn't quite ready to say, "I do."

"I don't think we should get in a hurry and announce anything just yet," she said when he finally got a break and called at mid-afternoon.

Donovan heard the slight coolness in her voice and knew that in the ten hours since he'd left her, she'd done some serious thinking. Even though he'd expected some degree of regret, he hadn't expected her to outright balk at announcing their relationship.

"We've waited seventeen years. I don't think that's getting in a hurry."

"I know." He heard her sigh. "I really hate to be the wet blanket, but we have to be sensible. Smart."

"Coming back here for you was the smartest thing I ever did," he said, his voice betraying his frustration and growing irritation. "Last night proves it."

"Good sex can't be the only basis for a relationship. There has to be more. I learned the hard way that marrying without love is the wrong thing to do."

"I love you," he said. "I—" His voice broke off. She'd never said it. "But you don't love me. What was it, Lara? Were you just curious to see if the real thing was as good as the memories?"

"I don't know what I feel for you," she said, and he heard the ring of an uneasy truth in the words. "I've thought I loved you. Convinced myself of it. And you're right. Last night was fantastic. If I believed that that's all love was, I wouldn't hesitate. But as much as we might want the sex to be all that's important, it isn't. As much as we might want things to be the same, they aren't. And as often as we tell ourselves we haven't changed, we have.''

"Not that much," he said. "Not in any way that matters."

"We can't know that!" she cried.

He heard the futility in her voice, the desperation to make him understand. Oh, he understood, okay. He understood the bottom line. His joy began to crumble around him.

"We've had—what?" she said, before he could formulate an argument. "Two or three real conversations since you've been back. And most of that was about the past. Then we went and complicated things by sleeping together."

"So you do regret it."

"Yes," she said, her voice harsh with remorse. "Under the circumstances, it was a foolish, irresponsible thing to do. We both should know better. And by the way, did you...use something?"

The question caught Donovan off guard. He wasn't irresponsible. Not usually. But this time he hadn't even thought about birth control. Placing the blame on the fact that it had been so long or that it happened so unexpectedly was no excuse. "No," he said at last. "But don't worry. Lightning doesn't strike twice in the same spot."

She gave a little cry of distress. "Darn you, Donovan! That's a myth, and you know it."

"Let's don't panic over something that might not happen," he told her. "And don't let your head talk your heart out of what you know is the truth."

"Truth? The truth is that we don't really know each other anymore, and I think we owe it not only to ourselves but to the other people our relationship will affect, to give these feelings some time to grow and develop, the way Sophie and Reed are doing.''

"Sophie and Reed are looking at houses," he reminded her. "Planning a wedding. They aren't giving it too much time.''

"We aren't Sophie and Reed, and they have special circumstances. They want to get Cassidy settled before school starts. And there's Belle."

"Belle and I will be fine."

"Maybe. As friends. But parenting is a whole other thing. As a live-in stepfather, you'd have rules.''

"I have rules now."

"Which is the point. She's going to be dealing with one new stepparent already. I just don't think it's fair to throw this at her right now.''

"You're seeing problems where there aren't any. Sophie and Reed—"

"Sophie and Reed have everything to gain and nothing to lose!" she said, her frustration getting the better of her.

A sudden, unexplained chill swept through Donovan. He didn't like the direction the conversation had just taken. "Meaning?"

"Meaning that I've worked like a dog to get where I am today."

"So we finally get to the real crux of the matter, don't we, Lara? This isn't about Belle. It's about you and your position in the community. Your job.''

"This is about all of us, can't you see that?"

"What I see is that you're at least right about one thing. People do change. You have. You used to not care about things like social standing.''

"I used to be naive about a lot of things," she said. Her voice had lost its edge of defeat and held a weary flatness. "But there's more than just me to think about now. I'm a single mom with a child to bring up. Yes, Reed is generous with his child support, and he's always there if I need something extra."

"Come on! You're filthy, stinking rich in your own right, Lara, so just stop with all the bull and cut to the chase!" he growled. "Let's be honest with each other. All your hemhawing around has nothing to do with how you feel about me and everything to do with your job."

"All right!" she cried, finally as angry as he. "You're right. That's part of it. Not all, but part. I do love you." The tenor of her voice softened, dropped to little more than a whisper. "At least I'm 99 percent sure it's love, but I've worked darn hard to get where I am, and I love my job, too. More important, I'm *good* at it, Donovan. I really believe I've made a difference in some kids' lives."

Donovan didn't answer. His own mind was in turmoil, wanting her to say what he wanted to hear, yet realizing that her pain was just as great because, for reasons he didn't understand, she couldn't.

"When Reed and I divorced, it almost cost me my position." She gave a short laugh. "I don't know why, but everyone seems to feel the high school principal and the local preachers should live perfect lives."

"They don't hang out with ex-cons, huh? And damn sure don't marry them."

He heard her draw in a sharp breath. "Don't do this."

"Do what?" he queried. "All I'm doing is laying it on the line the way you're so determined to do."

"Don't be angry," she pleaded.

"What should I be?"

"How about patient and understanding?"

His laughter was as bitter as wormwood. "My patience is about gone, Lara. And I think I understand real well."

"If I was never concerned about my social standing before, you were never short and sarcastic before," she commented. "Which proves my point. We've changed. We need to see how much, before we commit to saying we'll build a life together."

"You were never so concerned about the long term before."

"I was eighteen! I thought life held nothing but good. Now I know it can kick you in the teeth and that you have to be very careful if you don't want to lose everything."

"So we're back to the fact that you're afraid that if you see me openly, you'll lose your job."

He heard her utter a mild oath.

"Okay," she gritted out, evidently reaching the end of her own patience. "I am worried about my position, but believe it or not, it isn't just because you've spent time in prison. I'd feel the same way if I fell this fast for any man. I'm not willing to risk everything on one incredible night with you."

Donovan hadn't thought she could ever hurt him so badly. He'd been wrong. "Well, at least you admit it was incredible," he said with an attempt at levity.

"It was better than incredible," she said, the anger gone once again. "It was the most perfect night of my life, but I married in a hurry and for all the wrong reasons once, and I lived to regret it. I can't go through another divorce, and I won't put Belle through one, either."

"What makes you so sure it won't work?"

"What makes you so sure it will?" she countered. Silence hummed over the phone lines. "Look," she said at last, "listen to what I'm really saying, not to what you think you're hearing. I'm not saying no to you. I'm just saying we need to go slowly. We need to be sure."

Even though her choice hurt and he didn't want to admit it, Donovan understood where she was coming from. He even knew she was right. It didn't help the pain or lessen his anger.

"I am sure," he told her. "When you are, give me a call."

He'd hung up on her. Lara barely got the phone turned off before the tears began to fall. She hadn't expected him to be so unsympathetic to her very genuine fears. Maybe because he hadn't expected their roles to reverse.

She hadn't meant to hurt him, but she had to think of her future. She was older now. Smarter. More level-headed. She couldn't just think of herself. There was Belle. And they *had* changed. Things *were* different. Their phone conversation proved that. And, as much as she might want to take Donovan up on his offer and send the engagement announcement to the paper, she knew she had to make him see that the wisest thing to do was to take things slowly and do what they hadn't done before—date.

Are you ready to be seen out in the open with him?

Lara brushed away the troublesome thought like a fly on a piece of pie. She wouldn't think about that just now. First things first. She'd feel Belle out about the possibility of her dating someone, then mention Donovan and gauge her daughter's reaction. As for

Donovan, well, she'd give him some time to cool off, and the first chance she had, she'd go out and try to talk some sense into him. Depending on what happened, she'd go from there.

Belle's face wore a troubled expression. "Date? Why are you asking me if you can date someone? You've dated guys before without asking me."

It was later that evening, and after hours of pep talks, Lara had bolstered her courage enough to broach the subject with her daughter. A speculative gleam entered Belle's eyes.

"You don't just want to date anybody, or you wouldn't ask. You want to date someone in particular—right?"

Lara shrugged, striving for nonchalance. "Not necessarily."

Belle grinned. "You can't fool me. You've got a crush on someone. Who is it?"

A crush! Lara smothered a flutter of panic. The night she'd spent with Donovan could hardly be categorized as a crush. Now Belle was demanding to know who she wanted to date. Oh, well, in for a penny, in for a pound.

"It's your boss." Belle frowned and opened her mouth to say she didn't have a boss, when Lara clarified it for her. "Donovan."

"Donovan?"

The shock on Belle's face might have been comical if Lara hadn't been so worried about her response. Lara nodded.

"You want to date Donovan Delaney?"

Lara nodded again.

Belle's frown vanished, and she smiled broadly. "Cool."

The breath Lara hadn't been aware she was holding whooshed from her body in a loud sigh. One hurdle passed.

"You don't mind?"

"Why would I mind? Donovan's great." The frown returned. "I didn't know you knew each other that well."

Lara felt the heat of a blush creep into her face. "Oh. Well, we knew each other a long time ago. He used to do yard work for us and Aunt Isabelle." The truth, as far as it went. There was no reason to tell Belle any more than necessary. Lara forced a smile. "I had a crush on him back then."

"Really?"

Belle propped her elbows on the table and rested her chin in her palms. "Did he like you back?"

"Uh, yeah," Lara said, again opting for a condensed version of the truth. "We…saw each other a couple of times before he went to prison. Did you know about that?"

"Sure. I've talked to Sophie about it. She told me what happened, that Donovan accidentally shot their dad because he was drunk and trying to hurt her."

"Right." Despite the loneliness and pain she'd suffered, and in spite of the fact that the lie had unnecessarily separated them for so many years, Lara felt a bittersweet pride in the fact that he'd taken his sister's punishment. Donovan Delaney was that rare creature: an honorable man. She'd be a fool to let him slip away from her again.

"Does he know you like him?" Belle asked, bringing her thoughts back to the conversation at hand.

Another memory of the night flashed through Lara's mind. "Oh, I think he has a pretty good idea," she said. "I just wanted to see how you felt about it before the subject came up."

"So you don't have anything planned?"

All I have planned is to try to make him see reason—somehow.

"No, and I'd appreciate it if you didn't say anything to him about this conversation," Lara said. "You know men like to do the asking. They like to do the chasing."

"Mom. Times have changed. It's okay for you to make the first move."

"Maybe. But it isn't my style."

Belle rolled her eyes. "Whatever."

Lara went to the freezer to take something out to thaw for dinner.

"Hey, Mom," Belle said.

Lara turned. "Yes, baby?"

"What if you and Donovan got married?"

Lara's mouth dropped open.

"Well, if you really like each other, it could happen, couldn't it?"

Again, Lara strove for composure, which was hard with a million butterflies churning in her stomach. "I suppose, but—"

"That'd be so cool! Donovan would be my stepdad and my uncle, and Sophie would be my stepmom and my aunt." She laughed. "And Cassidy and I would be stepsisters and cousins! Wow."

Lara laughed, too, but all she could think of was that so far, every argument she'd made to Donovan for slowing things down was being struck down by a young girl's uncomplicated logic.

* * *

By Tuesday evening Reed and Sophie had made a decision on a house—sort of. They'd spent two hard days looking before finding one just down the street from Lara that they were seriously considering. Lara's neighborhood was the oldest and most prestigious in Lewiston, even though some of the houses had gone downhill in recent years. But recently the tide was changing because so many people wanted to get out of the larger cities. Lewiston had become a popular place to move to, and Oak Hill was seeing a lot of renovations.

Like Lara's, the house Sophie and Reed were considering was an old one, a two-story Queen Anne, built at the turn of the century. Like Lara's, it was in need of some major fixing up. Before making the final decision, they were frantically trying to track down plumbers, electricians and carpenters to get bids on repairs and renovations. If the bids and completion times were decent, they figured they could store Sophie's things, and she and Cassidy could live in the small guest house with Reed for a couple of months.

Even though they weren't committing themselves verbally, Lara could tell by the ecstatic look in Sophie's eyes that they'd found the right house. Lara had worn that same look when she'd found her own house and been filled with visions of what it would look like fully restored. The glazed look in Reed's was a giveaway, too. At this point, he'd do anything to make Sophie happy, even though he knew he could build a new house for what it would take to restore the old one.

Belle had always loved the house, which had a small conservatory at the back, and she was thrilled at the thought of having Cassidy within walking distance. Lara agreed that it would make things convenient, though she wasn't sure how Cassidy felt about that possibility, and she was less sure how she liked the idea of having Reed and Sophie close enough to know her every move. She was certain they felt the same way.

On the brighter side, they were three blocks down. Maybe they would come into the neighborhood from Elm Street and not pass by every time they came or went. At any rate, it was half-decided that they'd found the right house, and Reed was taking everyone to Texarkana for Italian to celebrate.

Lara decided that with Belle gone, it would be a good time to drive out and talk to Donovan. He'd had enough time to get over the worst of his anger, and it was time to go and try to mend some fences.

"Where are you going?" Belle asked, seeing that Lara had opted for a loose-flowing floral-print dress instead of her usual shorts after her shower.

Lara felt like a kid caught with her hand in the cookie jar. "Uh, nowhere important. I thought I'd drive over and pick up some things at Wal-Mart."

"You're awfully dressed up for Wal-Mart."

"I'm not dressed up," Lara said more sharply than she intended. "It's just a cotton dress."

A bit of the joy went out of Belle's face at hearing Lara's tone. Immediately contrite, Lara crossed the room and gave Belle a tight squeeze. "Sorry. I don't know why I'm so crabby."

"You've been a grouch ever since you told me you wanted to date Donovan," Belle complained, pulling free.

Thank goodness she didn't know the real reasons, Lara thought. "I'm sorry."

"Maybe you should just go see him and tell him how you feel," Belle suggested, her face brightening. It fell just as quickly. "No. That would be chasing him, wouldn't it?"

"Yes," Lara said, wanting to bring back Belle's smile. "But sometimes there are exceptions. I mean, he should at least have some idea I'm interested, right?"

"Right."

Lara gave what she hoped was a nonchalant shrug. "Maybe I will drive out and see him. I could tell him my shrubs need spraying again...or something."

"Good idea, Mom!"

A horn honked, and Lara glanced at her watch. Reed was running late. He was usually a stickler for being on time and coming to the door. Lara smiled. Evidently the new women in his life were playing havoc with his punctuality. Lara couldn't see Sophie being late for anything, but a teenage girl was a different matter altogether. It was something Reed would have to get used to.

Lara went with Belle to the front door. Reed's Lexus sat at the curb. Yep. He'd already picked up Sophie and Cassidy. The fact that he hadn't realized it would make more sense to pick up Belle before driving all the way out to Donovan's said something about the state of Reed's mind. Welcome to the wonderful world of blended families. For purely selfish reasons Lara was glad Reed had picked up Belle last. She wouldn't have to wait before she left for Donovan's place. She kissed Belle and waved and smiled at the trio in the car.

She watched until they turned the corner, then, closing the door, she looked at herself in the hall mirror, fluffing her hair and nodding with approval. The scoop-necked, floral dress was casual, unpretentious, but very feminine with its dainty buttons secured by fabric loops marching down the front. For once, her hair was behaving, and her makeup was perfect, if she did say so herself. She drew in a deep, fortifying breath. She was as ready as she'd ever be.

Donovan's Explorer was in front of the house, and his big white truck was parked out near the row of partially completed greenhouses. There were no other vehicles, so she assumed he was alone.

Fighting the bevy of butterflies cavorting in her stomach, she parked her own car and went to the front door, admiring the profusion of wildflowers growing in the bed along the front of the house. Two oversize, terra-cotta pots flanked either side of the steps and were filled to overflowing with a combination of plants—something tall and spiky, caladiums, impatiens and a variegated vinca. An artillery fern hung from a rafter, and a wicker basket filled with some sort of vine she didn't recognize sat on a small primitive table next to an equally old rocker. Donovan's handiwork.

There was no doorbell, so she knocked. No one answered. Had he seen her drive up and intended to ignore her? No, that wasn't his style. Donovan Delaney faced things head-on. Listening carefully, she heard the sound of music coming from somewhere inside the house. She knocked again. Still no answer.

Taking her courage and the doorknob in hand, Lara opened the door and poked her head inside. There was no sign of him in the living area. She stepped inside and glanced toward the kitchen-dining area. Empty.

She called his name again and still received no response. Then, faintly, she heard him from somewhere in the back of the house. Singing. Feeling like a thief, Lara eased down the hall, peeking into two bedrooms along the way. Both were obviously occupied by women. The last room must be Donovan's, she thought, making her way down the hall. The closer she got, the louder the music became. She heard water running. Donovan was in the shower, singing. And very well, too.

His room was exactly as she expected it. She wandered inside, touching things as she went. An antique bedroom suite that had probably belonged to his mother. A plain oak armoire. Tab curtains in sage-green-and-tan plaid at the window. Rag rugs on the polished pine floor. An exquisite bear-claw quilt on the bed, and half a dozen framed and matted autumn leaves, their scientific names written along with their common name hanging between the tall posts. More green plants. Modest, but artistic. Like the man who inhabited the space.

She was so busy soaking up her impressions of the room, she didn't hear the water being shut off or the rustle of the shower curtain. It was only when she heard whistling that she wheeled around. Donovan stood in the doorway.

She swallowed hard, the butterflies churning. She didn't know if she was nervous because he'd caught her trespassing or because he was so gorgeous. The towel he was using to dry his chest was the only thing that stood between his nakedness and her appraising eyes. He was tall and muscular without being bulky.

His legs were long and well formed, and his wide chest was covered with a riot of softly curling dark hair. His modesty was protected—barely—by the towel, which he'd used on his damp, mussed hair. It certainly wasn't the first time she'd seen him unclothed, but it was a sight that never failed to impress and please.

"What are you doing here?" he asked, breaking the silence.

Too bemused to resort to coyness, she answered truthfully. "I've been miserable. I thought I'd come and…see if we could talk."

In a quick move, he lowered the towel and wrapped it around his hips, giving her a brief flash of pure masculinity. He crossed his arms over his chest. "So talk."

"Your attitude isn't making this easy for me."

"Why should I make it easy for you? You aren't exactly making things easy for me, either."

She sighed. He was going to be difficult. Maybe a more direct approach would work better. She gave him a wan smile. "You seem awfully chipper for someone who claims to be heartbroken because I won't…marry you."

"Life has taught me that you can't change things, Lara," he told her. "And it goes on, no matter what. I'm sorry if my not wallowing in despondency over our little disagreement upsets you, but I'm just not an abject-misery kind of guy."

His directness was almost her undoing. Lara fought the urge to run from the room. Maybe coming out here was a mistake. Maybe she should have waited, let him make the first move. Maybe Aunt Isabelle was right, times hadn't changed that much, and men really did like to do the chasing. Maybe. But she was here and she'd try to finish what she came for…if only she could remember what that was, which was hard with him standing there looking so incredibly male.

"I had a talk with Belle."

Was that a flicker of surprise in his eyes?

"I told her I wanted to date you. She didn't seem to mind." Another attempt at a smile. "In fact, she gave her stamp of approval."

There was no discernible reaction from Donovan.

Lara felt her uncertainty give way to the first stirrings of irritation. She could tell him that Belle even sanctioned marriage between them, but faced with his unyielding attitude, she had no intention of eating that much crow.

"I'm trying to tell you that I'm taking steps to deal with the problems that might arise from our relationship."

He drew his heavy eyebrows together in a frown and sauntered to within two feet of her. "Our relationship?" he said in her face. "In case you don't know it, Lara, a one-night stand does not a relationship make."

She gasped at the blunt ruthlessness of his statement. She felt the blood drain from her face, then return with the heat of anger. "It wasn't just a one-night stand."

"No? What was it, then? You claim you don't know what you feel for me, so all I can assume is that it was nothing more than sex for you."

Lara didn't think; she reacted. She'd always thought that a woman slapping a man was clichéd, a ridiculous act that served little purpose but to make the woman look like a fool; nevertheless, for the second time since

Donovan had come back to town, she saw her hand
snake out and make stinging contact with his cheek.

Donovan grabbed her wrist and jerked her so close
she could feel the hardness of his thighs pressing
against hers. For long moments he stood there glaring
down at her while Lara watched his cheek turn red and
wondered how her plan had gone so miserably wrong.
Tears stung beneath her eyelids. She didn't want to
fight with him. She wanted to love him.

With a cry of capitulation, she surged against him,
raising herself on tiptoe and twining her free arm
around his neck to drag his head down.

Donovan's open mouth crashed against hers with a
bruising intensity. Intent on the bottom line, neither
had time for niceties. Between kisses and repeated dec-
larations of love from Lara, Donovan made short work
of the row of tiny buttons. The towel puddled in the
floor on top of her dress. Lara learned that his bed was
firm yet soft, like his flesh. This time he thought to
protect her, but she realized she really didn't care.

She loved him and wanted to be with him. Always.
The thought drew a sharp little breath. There was no
use denying it any longer. Whatever problems there
might be with her job could be worked out, somehow.
But not now. Not now.

Chapter Eight

Later Lara pressed a kiss to Donovan's chest, tipped her head back to look at him and said, "I'm starving."

He raised his head, angled his neck and managed to kiss her forehead. "I have some TV dinners and a really good bakery pie," he told her.

Lara gave a little shudder. "I've hardly eaten since you left the other day. I want real food."

"There are some steaks and stuff in the freezer I bought to fix for Sophe and Cassidy, but they'll take time to thaw."

"I'm starving *now*. Let me take you to this place way out in the country. A couple from Louisiana built it. It's on the river and fairly new, and they serve the best Cajun food this side of Lafayette, Louisiana."

"Sounds good," Donovan said, but his voice didn't hold much enthusiasm.

Lara recognized the problem immediately. Donovan

assumed she wanted to take him someplace out of the way to avoid seeing someone she might know. While she wouldn't deny that keeping things under wraps for a while was a prime consideration, that hadn't been on her mind when she'd made the suggestion. She raised herself up on one elbow and met his stony gaze with one of tender pleading. "It isn't what you think."

"Isn't it? What is it, then?"

"Really good Cajun food."

"Okay. Let's grab a shower and go have some."

As he started to roll away, she grabbed his arm. He collapsed back against the pillows.

"Cut me some slack here, Delaney," she said. "I came crawling out here to you, my tail tucked between my legs, so to speak, after you walked out of my life. I've admitted I love you, and I do. I don't think either of us could change enough to alter that, but yes, I do have concerns, and if you'd try to see things from my perspective, you'd understand what I'm going through."

Donovan turned his head back to meet her earnest gaze. "I haven't thought of much else the last couple of days," he told her. His smile looked more like a scowl. "Believe me there isn't much else to do when you're putting up shade cloth in the sweltering sun. You're right. I've been thinking about me. How I deserve to be happy with you and Belle."

"You do deserve it. We both do. And I am trying to work through things in small ways. I did talk to Belle about you. She adores you, and she's fine with it."

"Good," Donovan said. "But you're right. She needs time to adjust to the changes in her life Reed and Sophie's marriage will make."

"She also gave her approval for our marriage."

"She did?"

When Lara related Belle's comments about his, Sophie's and Cassidy's dual roles in her life if a marriage took place, he smiled. "Sharp kid. But she still needs some time. And you're right. We do, too."

"I think so."

"I don't want to sneak around, though, Lara."

The expression on her face grew serious. "Me, either. I'm not ashamed of you or what you are, Donovan. Believe me, but—"

"Ah," he said. "I thought I heard a but coming."

"Just a small one. There's a guy who moved here at mid-term last year. He's from a bigger city where he was an assistant principal. His résumé looks fantastic, and he has far more education and experience than I do."

"So why did he move to Lewiston?"

"His wife is the new doctor at the clinic. He had to tag along after her, I guess."

"Oh."

"The thing is, he didn't waste any time letting people know he'd like the principal's position, and there are still a few people who think a man would do a better job. I'm coming up for review by the school board in a couple of weeks. I think my work will stand the test, if I don't give Marcus Covington any ammunition to use against me—like me conducting a clandestine affair with the new guy in town."

"The ex-con."

"An affair with *anyone* would look bad. I'm supposed to be setting an example for the children of Lewiston. But you're right. In this town an affair with an ex-con is worse. Are you happy now that I've admitted it?''

"No," he said. "I'm not happy about any of it, but you have admitted that it's part of the problem, and I can deal with that as long as I know you aren't trying to deceive yourself.''

She laid her palm against his cheek and leaned over to kiss him. At first there was no reciprocal response, but finally, she felt his hand at the back of her head as he returned her kiss.

"I don't want to deceive anyone," she told him when she drew away. "But if we can just keep a lid on things until the board gives me their stamp of approval, I'll shout our relationship from the rooftops." She smiled. "Well, maybe not literally, but I'll date you openly. How's that?''

Donovan's steady gaze bore into hers while his thumb grazed the fullness of her lower lip. Lara dipped her head and curled her tongue around his thumb, her eyes pleading for understanding.

"A couple of weeks, huh?''

"Yes. Then no more secrecy, I promise.''

"Okay," he said at last. "You got it. Two weeks.''

Lagniappe, as the restaurant was called, was built in the typical Cajun style, with the roofline extending to cover the long porch. In this case, there were porches on the front and back where people could—weather permitting—sit while they waited for a table.

The rear porch looked over a particularly pretty spot on the river, complete with a five-foot waterfall with leaning trees on the opposite bank that seemed to be protecting the scene beneath them. Ferns sprouted from rocky crevices and between roots exposed by erosion. So far the area had received plenty of rain, and, though it was midsummer, the miniature waterfall made a satisfactory showing while lulling the viewers to restfulness with its peaceful rushing sound.

Donovan and Lara sat in twin woven-seated rockers, their hands locked between them, while a dozen other people milled about the porch and the herb garden that comprised much of the backyard area. He was as relaxed as he'd been since returning to Lewiston. Until now he hadn't realized just how much pressure he'd been under. As nonchalant as he appeared to the world, he was concerned about the town's reception of him. How could he not be? And there was so much to do with the greenhouses before he would be fully operating. All that while tackling the increasing number of landscape jobs that came his way.

Donovan spied a raccoon across the river above the falls as it washed something in the clear, rushing water. Silently he nudged Lara and pointed toward the masked bandit. She smiled in delight. So far, he was impressed by the place. A connoisseur of Cajun food and not half-bad when it came to cooking it, he would reserve judgment on the cuisine.

He closed his eyes and rested his head against the rocker's high back. He was glad he'd come, if for no reason than that it prolonged his time with Lara. Finally she'd said she loved him. Not once, but over and over. He had to believe her. Wanted to. Just as he wanted to believe she was being honest with him about the upcoming school board review. While he wasn't thrilled with their deal, it was a step in the right direction. He only hoped that when the two weeks were up, she didn't find another excuse to keep their relationship a secret.

The sound of the restaurant's door opening pushed that uneasy thought from his mind. He heard footsteps on the boards as someone exited the building.

"Well, hello, Lara. I never expected to see you here."

Donovan's eyes flew open as Lara dropped his hand. A handsome, aging man stood next to her chair. Rowland Hardisty. He glanced at Donovan, his smile benign, a direct dichotomy to his shrewd, thoughtful expression.

"Hello, Rowland," Lara said, the slight quaver in her voice betraying a hint of nervousness. "I didn't expect to see you here."

She tucked a strand of hair behind her ear in a gesture that betrayed her anxiety. Donovan understood her unease. Reed's father was a commanding presence. Always had been. And there was something intimidating about the way he looked at you. Just now that look was aimed at Lara, but Donovan knew her former father-in-law was taking note of the closeness of their chairs and the fact that they were sitting side by side.

"I try to eat sensibly," he said, "but every now and then, I get a hankering for something spicy. This is a good place to satisfy that craving. I can't believe I ran into you. If I hadn't wanted to come out and look at the herb garden, I'd have missed you, and that would have been a shame."

Donovan didn't miss the double meaning of Rowland's comment.

"Reed has Belle for the evening," Lara said by way of explanation. "I didn't want to cook, so I decided to treat myself to an evening out."

So that's the way it would be, Donovan thought with a sinking heart. Though Rowland might suspect as much, she had no intention of letting Reed's dad know they were there together. It hurt, but they had made an agreement, and Donovan would do his best to hold up his end of it, even though it half killed him.

"I can recommend the gumbo. It was delicious, as usual." Rowland said, turning that deliberate gaze fully Donovan's way.

"Hello, Donovan."

"Dr. Hardisty."

"How's the new business going?"

"As well as can be expected. Lots of work to do yet."

"I'm sure there is. So you're having a night out, too?"

"Yep. Reed took Sophie and Cass out, and I'd heard this was a good place. Lara and I were just saying how we could have come together if we'd known we were both stranded for the evening." The lie stuck in his craw, even though Donovan told himself it was for a good cause, and, as lies went, a pretty good one.

Rowland's smile said he suspected the ruse was just that. "Well, I hope you both have a good evening and enjoy your dinner."

"Thanks," they said in unison. Rowland gave a little wave and crossed the porch to the steps that led to the garden.

"Thanks for playing along," Lara said lowly, taking Donovan's hand in a tight grip. "As if he doesn't mess in my life enough as it is, Rowland happens to be on the school board."

"I aim to please," Donovan said with an uneven smile.

He cast a look toward Rowland, who was almost to the corner of the restaurant. Without warning the door opened and a hostess stepped outside. "Delaney," she bellowed. "Party of two. Your table's ready."

From where he sat Donovan noticed two things. Lara's eyes widened in horror, and Rowland Hardisty stopped dead in his tracks. He paused no longer than a couple of seconds before moving out of sight, but long enough for Donovan to be certain he'd heard the hostess's announcement. Rowland didn't have to turn and see if Lara and Donovan went inside together. He knew.

"It was one of the most horrible moments of my life," Lara said to Wes a few days later. He'd stopped by on his way to the grocery store and they were out by the pool, sipping fresh-squeezed lemonade. Lara was stretched out in a lounger; Wes, filled with nervous energy as usual, was pacing the pool's perimeter. In accordance with her promise to Donovan to rid their relationship of obstacles, she'd confessed to her ex-husband and her brother that she and Donovan were again seeing each other in secret. Reed was fine with the news and glad Belle was so accepting. He understood her reluctance to be open about the relationship, but said he didn't think Donovan was the kind of man who could be put off very long.

Wes didn't seem too surprised, though it was clear he thought she was crazy for keeping things secret. "What did Donovan have to say?"

"He went along with the lie, but I know it didn't sit well with him." Her misery-filled gaze met her brother's. "I think it would be safe to say that running into Rowland put a damper on the evening."

"No doubt," Wes said with his customary bluntness. He shoved his fingers through his hair and pinned her with a disgusted look. "You would think you'd have learned something from the past."

"And what is that supposed to mean?"

"You and Donovan did this sneaking-around routine as kids. You're both intelligent, successful adults, fully capable of deciding who you want to spend your time—your lives—with. You don't owe any explanation to Rowland Hardisty or anyone else in this town."

"Maybe not, but he's my ex-father-in-law and Belle's grandfather as well as being on the school board. I'm sure you haven't forgotten all I went through to get my job, or that Rowland was one of my biggest detractors."

"No, I haven't," Wes said. "But it can't compare to the hell you and Donovan have been through being apart all these years. Now that you have a chance for the thing you've always wanted, I can't believe you're putting some stupid job first. We don't often get second chances to make things right, Sis. You ought to know that."

The accusation hit Lara hard. For Wes to claim she'd put it ahead of her love for Donovan hurt. Still, she couldn't stifle either the niggling feeling that he was right or the fear that if she let this opportunity to build a life with Donovan slip from her grasp, she'd never get a third chance.

"That isn't fair," she said. "I've worked hard, and I've done a good job."

Wes squatted beside her lounge chair and looked her in the eye. "And the people in this town know it," he said earnestly. "But your ridiculous stipulation isn't fair to Donovan or you. It seems to me you had more guts as a kid."

"I told you, it's only until after the board meeting. I'm older and wiser now, Wes."

"Are you?"

"What do you mean?"

Wes threw his hands into the air. "Look at us! You're thirty-four years old. I'm thirty-six. I can't sustain a meaningful relationship with a woman for more than two months at a stretch because I'm always analyzing whether or not it will work instead of letting the relationship develop.

"You're divorced. You couldn't make it with Reed because you were pining for Donovan. Now you have a chance for the thing you've always wanted, and you're about to throw it away because some narrow-minded people in this podunk town might disapprove? Tell me, little sister, how wise is that?"

"The meeting is just over a week away," she pointed out.

"Just over a week away? Take a look at the past, Sis," Wes pleaded. "A lot of things can take place in nine days. Look at Reed and Sophie and how fast that happened. Or Dad's heart attack. He was okay one day, dead the next. If you really love Donovan, you've got to have the courage to stand by him, no matter what his past is or what it does to your damned career, because I'm telling you, we don't have any promise of tomorrow."

Donovan was sitting out on the porch, watching the dust from Jett's disappearing truck fog the nearby fields when Sophie came outside with a glass of sweet tea and a platter of fresh-baked chocolate-chip cookies.

"What's the occasion?" he asked, taking the proffered glass.

"You've seemed depressed the last couple of days. I thought some endorphins might help."

"Aren't you afraid I'll ruin my supper?" he asked, picking up a cookie.

She rolled her eyes and sat down in the swing next to him. "A growing boy like you? Besides, Reed can't get here for another hour and a half."

Donovan grinned. "So my meals are now at the mercy of your love life, huh?"

"Hey," she said as he took a bite of the cookie. "I'm cooking."

He chewed and swallowed. "You're right. Please accept my apology." He polished off three more cookies without speaking. "So have you decided on the house?"

"Yeah. We just got the final bids. It's going to cost a lot to fix it up, but we'll really have something when we're finished, so we decided to take it. Reed says he thinks we can be in by fall."

"Think you can stand living so close to Rowland for that long?"

Sophie grimaced. "It won't be easy. Evidently he and Reed had a set-to the other day about some things Rowland said to Cassidy."

Donovan's hand clenched around the glass. "If I ever hear him say anything to hurt her, I'll clean his clock."

Sophie smiled and gave his arm a sisterly pat. "My hero. Actually, I think you'd have to take a number. Reed's doing an excellent job of defending the honor of the women in his life."

"I'm glad to hear it."

"So what's up with you and Lara? I know you haven't seen her in a few days."

"It's hard to have a relationship when you're sneaking around."

"Why *are* you sneaking around? You're consenting adults."

The expression in Donovan's eyes grew hard. "Because it's what the lady wants."

Sophie's eyes widened in surprise. "Are you serious?"

"Do I look like a guy who's kidding?"

"But why?"

"Bottom line? She's afraid if word gets out she's seeing me, she'll lose her job."

Sophie muttered a very uncharacteristic curse. "It isn't fair."

He shrugged. Vocalizing the situation brought home the seriousness of things and pushed Donovan even deeper into his pit of depression. He reached for another cookie. "She says it's just for a couple of weeks, and then we'll tell the world."

"But you don't believe her."

"I don't know what to believe. I just know I don't like it."

"Give her an ultimatum—you or the job."

Donovan slanted her a wry glance. "Am I hearing right? Is Ms. Compromise really telling me to deliver an ultimatum?"

"Sometimes it's the best course of action. Either you're more important than her job, or you aren't. In which case, you wouldn't want to be tied to her, anyway."

The statement deepened the misery in Donovan's blue eyes. The thought of coming so close to the brass ring and not being able to grab on to it was more than he thought he could bear. But he knew Sophie was right. He would rather live the rest of his life alone than be tied to a woman who thought more of her job than she did him.

"You're right, but it's hard, you know?"

"I know." They swung in silence for a few minutes, the only sounds the creaking of the chain and the chitter of warring hummingbirds at the feeder. "So what are you going to do?"

Donovan exhaled a heavy sigh. "Give her until the meeting and see what happens."

"Have you talked to her at all?"

"No."

"Reed says she's sick. Some kind of flu bug."

"Maybe I'll call and check on her."

"Maybe you should." After a few minutes Sophie said, "I saw Aunt Opal at the dollar store today."

"How is she?"

"She looks terrible and says the pain is getting worse. I'm surprised she's still able to get out and about."

"I can't believe she's dying and Justine's too busy with her singing career to come home to see her."

"Justine's pregnant," Sophie said, bluntly.

It was Donovan's turn to be surprised. "Are you serious?"

Sophie nodded. "You don't watch those gossip shows on TV?"

He shook his head. "I saw something on one of those supermarket tabloid covers, but I figured it was just gossip or some publicity stunt."

"No. It's true."

"Who's the father?"

"She isn't saying."

"Maybe I'll give her a call," Donovan said.

"Be my guest. I'm certainly not having any luck. She said she isn't sure she'll be here for the wedding. That really hurt."

"I'm sure it did," Donovan said, knowing firsthand how close the two had once been. "I'll give her a call, later. I used to be able to sweet-talk her into about anything, and it isn't as if illegitimate babies don't happen every day. It's certainly no reason to stay away from your dying mother or your cousin's wedding."

"It's more than the pregnancy," Sophie said. "She's alluded to some grudge against Aunt Opal."

"Like what?"

"I don't know," Sophie said, "but whatever it is, it's serious."

Donovan's first call after dinner was to check on Lara. "This is Donovan," he said when Belle answered. "How's your mom feeling?"

"Not so good. She's asleep right now. Do you want me to wake her up for you?"

"No. Let her rest. Just tell her I called."

"Okay."

"And, Belle, call me if there's anything I can do."

"I will."

Donovan hung up, wishing he could go over and see her and hold her until she felt better. Would he be welcome, or would Lara worry that his truck would be seen by a neighbor?

"Sophie saw Aunt Opal today and says she's really getting bad," Donovan said when he called his cousin later that night.

There was a pause on the line. Finally Justine said, "I sent her some money."

"She doesn't want your money," Donovan thundered. "She wants to see you."

"Don't yell at me!"

Donovan thought he heard the threat of tears in Justine's voice. "I'm sorry, but I think you're making a huge mistake. I don't know what happened between you, but she's your mother, and you wouldn't be here without her. So she made some mistakes. We all do. From what Sophie says, you have."

He heard Justine suck in a shocked breath.

"That wasn't a dig, Juss, just a fact. Your pregnancy is your business. What I'm saying is that I'm not a parent and may never be, but I've watched Sophie and Cass. Sophie is a good mom, but even with a degree in psychology, she's made her fair share of mistakes. It happens. Things happen. You deal with it."

"You don't know what she did."

Definitely tears, Donovan thought. "No I don't. But I've been through some tough times, and I've learned some important lessons. I truly believe we're given adversity to test our mettle. I even believe that if we don't learn the lesson we're supposed to, God keeps sending us the same problem in different guises until we do. I know for sure that we can't let the poison of disappointment and defeat eat at us, because if we do, we're robbing ourself of the capacity to grow and, what's more important, to love."

He heard her sniff even as she made an attempt at sarcastic humor. "When did you get your psych degree? You sound like Sophie."

"Osmosis, I guess," he said, smiling himself. At least she was listening. "So will you come?"

"I'll think about it."

Donovan stifled a sigh. It wasn't what he wanted to

hear, but it was more than he expected. "Fair enough," he told her. "Just don't wait too long."

At midnight Donovan was still awake, worrying about Lara. Muttering a curse, he got up, pulled on some clothes and let himself out into the balmy night. Like it or not, he was going to see how she was doing.

He parked in her driveway and, praying there were no man-eating dogs roaming the neighborhood, he slipped through the shadows to the side of the house where her downstairs bedroom was situated. Skinny fingers of a light poked through the horizontal slats of the blinds. Easing to the window, being careful not to trample any plants, he rapped sharply on the glass, waited and knocked again.

Finally the blind was raised, and Lara peered out at him. Even in the glow of the small bedside lamp, he could see she was pale. At first glance she could be mistaken for a teenager in her oversize, Tweety T-shirt. But the haunted expression in her eyes was very adult, and it tore at his heart.

Lips set, she unlocked the window and raised it, placing her hands on the sill. "What are you doing here?" she asked in a low, irritated whisper.

"I was worried about you."

The frown faded. "I'm feeling much better, thank you."

"So prim and proper," he murmured. "Move."

"What?"

"You heard me. Unhook the screen and move. I'm coming in."

"Donovan," she said, even as she did his bidding. "It's late."

"I know," he said, setting the screen aside and

clambering inside. "All the neighbors should be asleep, and I don't plan to stay long, so your reputation should be safe."

She laughed, a sound that caught on a little sob. "You think so?"

"I'm doing the best I can," he said, lowering the window and the blind.

"And I thought you hadn't called because you were angry with me."

"I was. Hell, maybe I am, but I missed you like crazy, and I couldn't stand the thought of you being sick and not being with you."

He reached out and pulled her into a close embrace. Her arms went around his neck, and his hands slid beneath her shirt to the softness hiding below. Her breath caught sharply.

"Besides," he said, "I figure I should take every opportunity to remind you that what we have is very special."

"Oh, Donovan!" She shook her head and said cryptically, "In for a penny, in for a pound." Then she reached for the hem of her T-shirt and stripped it over her head.

Out on the street the man in the car noted the truck in the driveway and saw the light in the back bedroom wink out.

Something awakened Belle. She lay stiffly in her bed, uncertain if she'd really heard something or if she was just dreaming. There it was again. Downstairs. Was her mom feeling bad again? Belle swung her legs over the side of the bed and made her way down the stairs and along the hall to her mother's room.

The door was closed, as it had been all day. Belle

reached out to open it but stopped when she heard Donovan's voice say, "You're so beautiful."

Her mother's reply was a little moan followed by other sounds. Belle felt her face grow hot. Her hand slid from the doorknob. She'd watched enough TV to understand what those sounds meant. Donovan and her mother were having sex!

Mortified at the thought and feeling betrayed—her mom said it was wrong unless you were married—Belle turned and crept stealthily back down the hall and up the stairs.

She'd watched films in sex education class and understood the general concept. It was hard to see what the big deal was, when the whole thing seemed pretty disgusting. She tried to imagine her mother and Donovan…no! She couldn't picture it. A new thought sprang into her mind. Was her dad having sex with Sophie?

Don't be naive, Belle. You've watched enough soap operas and seen enough movies that you know that grown-ups don't wait, even though they might tell you to. At least most of them didn't. Adults lived by double standards, she thought, seizing on the concept with fierce indignation. Preaching one thing and practicing another.

Belle climbed back into her bed and squeezed her eyes shut against the sudden burning of tears. Now she knew how Cassidy must have felt the morning she found out about the two of them having the same dad.

Chapter Nine

Lara was pouring batter into the waffle iron when Belle came down the next morning. "Morning, honey. Sleep well?"

"Better than you."

Lara cast a questioning glance over her shoulder. "Meaning?"

"Meaning I know you're sleeping with Donovan."

Lara froze, then set down the mixing bowl and turned slowly toward her daughter. "I beg your pardon?"

"There's no need to deny it. I heard the two of you last night."

"What do you mean, you heard us?"

Belle nodded. "I heard something and thought you were feeling bad again, so I came downstairs and I…heard you."

Lara closed her eyes. What else could happen? Ever

since she'd taken up with Donovan Delaney again, her nice, predictable life had been one of constant up-heaval and worry. She worried that someone would find out, worried whether it was the right thing—or the wrong thing to do—worried that she'd lose her job, that Belle would rebel. Now this!

"I'm sorry."

Belle fixed a piercing gaze on her that reminded her of Rowland. Belle was so much like Lara's side of the family, sometimes she forgot Hardisty blood flowed in her daughter's veins, too.

"Sorry that you did it, or sorry I found out?"

Lara knew it was a time to be completely honest. "Sorry you found out. You've had a lot to come to terms with lately. Now this."

Belle regarded her coolly for several seconds. "Well, at least you didn't lie about it."

"Lying is never the smart thing to do when there's something important at stake, and I think our relation-ship is very important," Lara said, choosing her words carefully.

"Why did you do it when you tell me sex is wrong outside of marriage?" Belle asked with a frown. "Isn't that a double standard?"

Lara nodded. "Yes, it is. I love him, Belle. That doesn't make it right, but it's the only excuse I have."

"Are you going to marry him?"

"We haven't gotten that far, but I've been thinking about it, yes. Do you still think it would be cool?"

Belle's gaze slid away. "I don't know," she said, and Lara knew Belle was still angry with her. And, she thought, rightly so.

Donovan and Jett, who was hung over and swearing he'd never touch another drop of beer, were unrolling plastic when the police car came down the lane. Donovan's heart slammed into his ribs—would he ever see a police car that he didn't feel instant worry?—but he managed to grin at the younger man. "What kind of mischief did you get into last night?"

Jett's eyes were wide. "Nothing. I swear."

The Lewiston police car pulled to a stop, and a man Donovan recognized from his school days got out. He and Jimmy French hadn't been good friends growing up, but Jimmy's family had been poor, too. Donovan remembered him as a quiet, honest kid with a tender heart. The honesty was the only attribute Donovan could see that would make him a likely candidate for law enforcement.

"Donovan," the man said with a nod, clearly uncomfortable with his mission.

"Hello, Jimmy." Donovan managed to sound pleasant and unconcerned, even though his insides were churning. "What can I do for you?"

"Is there some place we can talk privately?"

Donovan's lips tightened. So it wasn't Jett they were after. Donovan's heart sank with the realization that for the rest of his life whenever a crime was committed, he'd be the first one they thought to question.

"Sure," he said, getting down from the ladder. "Let's walk." He turned to Jett. "Why don't you take a break until I get back?"

Donovan and the policeman moved between two greenhouses and out of earshot. "What's up, Jimmy?" Donovan asked, making the first move.

"There was a rape in town last night," Jimmy said, not mincing words.

"And I'm automatically a suspect, right?" Donovan

said, feeling the cornerstone of his carefully reconstructed world shift.

Jimmy held out a hand. "Now don't get all mad at me, Donovan. I'm not taking you in or anything. But you know people with priors are the first ones we check out when something like this happens."

"I wasn't sent up for rape, Jimmy," Donovan clarified. "I killed someone—remember?"

Jimmy flinched at the bluntness of the statement. Again Donovan wondered how Jimmy had ever become a policeman. "Who was she?"

"What?" Jimmy seemed confused by the question.

"Who was the woman?" Donovan repeated.

"A high school cheerleader named Lexie Jamerson."

Donovan swore. Bud Jamerson, a guy who'd been ahead of him in school, and his wife, Peggy, had had a baby daughter a month or two before Donovan was arrested for shooting Hutch. They'd named her Alexa. No doubt they were one and the same. His heart throbbed painfully. He could only imagine the horror Bud and Peggy must be going through.

He swallowed hard. "Is she going to be okay?"

"As okay as she can be, considering," Jimmy said.

"Was she able to give you any information?"

"She was actin' real crazy and bawlin' and stuff," Jimmy said. "Doc Hardisty wouldn't let us talk to her just yet, said she'd been through enough. He gave her something to knock her out and told us to come back later."

Donovan was a bit surprised by Rowland Hardisty's kindness, even though it didn't help his situation.

"I didn't do it." Donovan gave the standard reply of every criminal who ever breathed.

"I know, but the chief wanted me to come out and talk to you. I just have a couple of questions."

Donovan fought the urge to turn and walk away. "Sure."

Jimmy took a small pad and a pen from his pocket. "Where were you last night?"

"Right here, most of the night," he said, recalling his late-night visit to Lara. Dear God! What would Lara think if she heard about the police paying him a visit?

"What time did you leave?"

Donovan remembered looking at the clock. "About midnight."

Jimmy frowned. *Beep!* Donovan thought. Wrong answer.

"Where did you go?"

"Into town."

The frown deepened. Another wrong answer. The rape had occurred in town or the sheriff would have come to question him.

"Were you with anyone?" Jimmy asked.

"Yeah," Donovan said. "A...friend."

Jimmy noticed the hesitation. His gaze sharpened. "A woman?"

Donovan realized that, with a certain desperate logic, Lexie Jamerson fit that description. Three strikes and you're out! "Yes, a woman."

"Do you mind if I ask who?"

All it would take was a simple corroboration from Lara, and he'd be off the hook. But Lara was adamant about no one knowing about their involvement until after the school board meeting. He'd promised her, and he meant to keep that promise. "I darn sure do."

The answer surprised Jimmy.

"I'm protecting the lady's privacy, Jimmy," Donovan explained. "That's all. I'm not hiding anything."

"Hey, I believe you, but the chief is a different matter. Is there any other way I can corroborate your whereabouts?"

Donovan scraped a hand through his hair, shook his head and met Jimmy's gaze steadily. "No. Are you taking me in?"

"Lord, no," Jimmy said. "But Chief Landers might want to talk to you again."

Donovan swore. "Look, do I need an attorney?"

Jimmy shrugged and put the notepad back into his pocket. "That's up to you, I guess."

When Jimmy left, Donovan told Jett what was going on.

"Lexie Jamerson?" he said, his face draining of color. "You're kidding!"

Jett looked as upset as Donovan felt. He shook his head. "Do you know her?"

"Sure I know her. We even dated a couple of times after she and Darren broke up." He rubbed at his eyes, as if he were trying to keep from crying. "Why did the cops come out to talk to you?"

"I have a record. Ergo, I may be guilty."

"That's a bunch of bull."

"Yeah, but it's the way things are," Donovan said.

"Man, I can't believe this."

Donovan didn't have the heart to tell his young helper that if he'd dated Lexie, he might be questioned by the authorities, too. "Why don't we call it a day," he said. "I'm not much in the mood for work right now."

Jett shook his head. "You take some time. I'll keep at it. Want me to come in tomorrow?"

"Fine," Donovan said. "I'll check on you later."

When Jett left, Donovan went inside to tell Sophie and Cassidy what was going on. Sophie's immediate reaction was to burst into tears.

"Come on, Sis," Donovan said, more irritated than upset. "We don't have time for this. I need to see what my rights are." He was wondering if the lawyer who'd represented him before was still practicing.

"This is so asinine," Cassidy said, crossing the room to her mother.

"Thanks, Cass."

She smiled, albeit weakly. "Why don't you call Reed?"

"Reed?"

"Yeah," Cassidy said. "You know? Reed. My dad."

Reed. Soon to be his brother-in-law. He was the logical person to consult, but Donovan was hesitant. "I'm afraid asking him to represent me might put a strain on our relationship just now," Donovan said.

"Represent you!" Sophie cried. "Do you think you're going to need representation?"

"It was just a figure of speech," Donovan said. "I don't know what's going to happen, but I want to be prepared. I haven't come this far to have everything go down the drain again." *Ah, Lara...Lara.*

"Why didn't you just tell him you were here."

"Because I wasn't," Donovan said. "At least not all night."

Sophie and Cassidy both wore surprised expressions. "Where were you?"

"You know, Sophe." He looked at Cassidy. "Sorry, Cass. It's a secret for now."

Instead of the anger he expected, Cassidy's face brightened. "It's a woman! You were with *her!*"

Getting Donovan married off to a special woman was Cassidy's dearest wish. "Yeah, I was with her," he said without any joy.

There was a speculative gleam in Cassidy's eyes. "That's why you came back here, isn't it?"

Donovan nodded. "We were seeing each other secretly when I got sent to jail. I broke it off, but I never got over her. And yes, she's the reason I came back, but for personal reasons she doesn't want anyone to know about us just now, so I can't say who she is."

"Oh," Cassidy said, her disappointment obvious.

Sophie, in control of her emotions once more, blew her nose on a tissue. "Cassidy is right," she said, trying to steer the conversation in a new direction. "Reed might not be the best person to talk to, but he'd be able to tell you who is. Call and have him come out."

"Good thinking."

"Don't panic, Lara," Reed said when he called his ex-wife's house just seconds after he and Donovan hung up. "But I thought you'd want to know that the Jamerson girl was raped last night, and the police have already been out to talk to Donovan."

Lara, who was still upset over her confrontation with Belle, thought she'd misunderstood. "I beg your pardon?"

"Lexie Jamerson was raped last night."

Lara rubbed at her temple where a sudden pain had begun to throb. Lexie was in summer school. She was the girl who'd been having trouble with her boyfriend the day Donovan first showed up. A feeling of déjà vu swept over her.

"Dear God!" she breathed. "Is she all right?"

"I haven't heard any details. Donovan called about the time Liz came in with the news."

"Am I missing something here?" Lara asked, confusion breaking through the shock of Reed's announcement. "I don't understand what this has to do with Donovan."

"Simple," Reed said. "He's been convicted of a previous crime, so the smart people who enforce our laws figure maybe he did this one, too. I call it small-mind mentality. You know Bobby Landers. He's not the sharpest knife in the drawer. He just happens to be one of the most charismatic people in town."

"Which is such an excellent reason to appoint him police chief," Lara said bitterly.

"Don't bite my head off. I didn't put him in office."

"I'm sorry. Surely they can't believe Donovan had anything to do with that."

"He doesn't exactly have an alibi," Reed said.

"What does that mean?"

"He says he was with someone—a woman—but he won't say who. I don't suppose you'd happen to know who she is, would you?"

"You know perfectly well if he was with a woman it was me," Lara said in a tart voice.

"I thought you were sick."

"I was. He came over a little past midnight to see how I was doing."

"How long was he there?"

Lara rubbed at her temple again. "Until around two, I think."

"Well, your secret is safe, because he isn't talking.

Look, I have to run. I told Donovan I'd come out and talk to him."

"Wait!" Lara said before he could hang up. "You might as well know that Belle—" her face turned scarlet "—heard us."

"Heard you? As in you and Donovan...together." She nodded and Reed sighed. "Great!"

"I'm sorry. She came down to check on me, and heard him in my room. Needless to say, she's pretty upset about my living a double standard."

"Well, she wasn't thrilled when I fell off my pedestal, either. Do you want me to take her with me?"

Lara brightened. "It might not hurt. Maybe she can cry on Cassidy's shoulder."

"Right," Reed said. "I'll be over to pick her up in a few minutes."

Reed arrived at the Delaney place within thirty minutes of Donovan's call to Reed, Belle in tow. Donovan smiled and spoke to her, and, though she responded, there was no reciprocal smile. Instead she just stood there with her hands in her pockets and looked up at him for several seconds with a considering expression on her face. Then Cassidy came out and they both disappeared into Cassidy's room so the adults could talk.

"She knows what happened?" Donovan asked, cocking his head toward the bedroom.

Reed nodded. "Bare bones only. I told her as we were driving out here. Sort of damage control."

"But why tell her, when it won't affect her? She doesn't know about me and Lara."

"Oh, but she does," Reed said, dropping the bombshell without any warning. "Besides, she's been spending a lot of time with you. Of course it affects her.''

"How did she find out?" Donovan asked.

"She heard you in Lara's room."

Donovan shoved his chair away from the table with so much force, it tipped over. Only his quick reaction saved it from crashing to the floor. "I knew going there was a stupid move, but I figured if anyone saw me, it would be a neighbor." He swore again and moved to look out the French doors at the pool. "This is exactly the kind of thing Lara wanted to avoid."

Sophie rose and went to him, placing a comforting hand on his shoulder. "There's no sense beating yourself up about it after the fact," she said. "She's a pretty smart little girl and very adult for her age. She'll work through this the same way she and Cassidy are working through what they found out about Reed and me."

"Maybe," Donovan said, "but she's had a lot thrown at her in a short time, things that would be hard for an adult to come to terms with, much less a kid."

"But she will come through it," Sophie said with her usual optimism. "She knows you, knows you'd never do something like rape."

Donovan nodded, though there wasn't much conviction in the action. He turned to Reed. "I didn't do it."

"Do I look stupid?" Reed asked.

Seeking solace, Donovan picked up a handful of the cookies Sophie had baked the day before and sat down at the table. "What should I do?"

"I wouldn't do anything just right now. I checked with Bobby. They still haven't questioned Lexie. Unless she points the finger at you, or they find something that ties you to the scene, they can't seriously consider you a suspect. Besides, if push comes to shove, I know you have an alibi."

Donovan and Sophie shot each other a startled glance.

"I spoke with Lara. She told me you were at her place from about midnight until two."

Donovan swore. "I'm not telling the cops about that. She needs us to lay low for a week or so yet, until after the school board meeting."

Reed shook his head. "I admire your loyalty, but don't be a martyr just to protect Lara's job."

"Believe me, I'm not in the martyr business, but unless they're snapping the handcuffs on to haul me off to jail, my lips are sealed."

"I have a pretend situation to ask you about," Belle said to Cassidy as she situated herself in the middle of the bed facing her newly found sister. "Remember the other one?"

"A hypothetical situation," Cassidy said. "And yes, I remember the other one." Cassidy had fabricated an elaborate story with a fictitious "she" when she'd first learned about Reed being her father as well as Belle's. "So what's the problem?"

"What if something bad happened and someone innocent got blamed for it?"

"Like how bad?" Cassidy asked. "Like someone breaking your mom's favorite vase and you getting blamed?"

Belle leaned forward, her face a study in grim entreaty. "No. Something really bad. So bad, he—I mean they—might have to go to jail."

The slip of Belle's tongue told Cassidy the younger girl was talking about the current situation with Donovan. "If you believe the person is innocent, then I guess all you can do is pray that somehow the truth will come out and the person who really committed the crime gets caught."

"What if you have mixed feelings about the person?"

Cassidy regarded Belle's tormented features. She knew Belle had been spending time with Donovan to learn the horticulture business, and so far as Cassidy knew, the two of them were getting along great. What could possibly have happened to change that?

"I'm not sure I understand," she said, hoping Belle would volunteer more information. "What kind of mixed feelings?"

Belle dropped her gaze to the floral bedspread and plucked at a petal repeatedly, as if she might actually pick it. "I like the person. I like them a lot. I thought we were friends, but he—I mean, they—betrayed our friendship."

"How?"

Belle lifted her tormented gaze to Cassidy's. "This is hard to explain."

It was amazing, Cassidy thought, how close she and Belle had grown in such a short time. The younger girl was the sister she'd always dreamed of having, and any pain Belle felt automatically became Cassidy's. She took Belle's hand in hers. "I'm not going anywhere."

"He betrayed me by…uh, I guess you could say he likes someone else better—someone who's really close to me. But that isn't quite it, either."

Cassidy's mind churned. *He,* the innocent person—

Donovan—had betrayed Belle by *liking* someone else better. Someone close to Belle. The pieces of the puzzle fell into place, supplying Cassidy a missing piece of her own. Donovan's special woman must be Lara Hardisty. Somehow Belle had found out the two of them were an item. Now Belle was jealous of her mom's relationship with Donovan. Well, maybe jealousy was too strong a word. Maybe there was more she didn't know.

"So you're upset because he likes this other person better?"

"No. I'm upset because they had sex."

Whoa! That was another kettle of fish altogether, and coming so close on the heels of Belle finding out her dad and Cassidy's own mother had had sex as teenagers was no doubt devastating. No wonder some kids rebelled. Parents expected certain behavior from their offspring, but they played by a completely different set of rules.

"I heard them," Belle said, before Cassidy could ask how she knew that for certain. Then, seeing that she'd said too much, Belle's face crumpled, and the tears began to fall.

Suddenly furious at her beloved uncle herself, Cassidy scooted closer to Belle and pulled her into a loose embrace.

"I heard them, Cassidy. In my mom's bedroom. Donovan and Mom. I *know* what they were doing."

Cassidy stroked Belle's hair and let her ramble, hearing things like "disgusting," "double standards," and "hate them both." Cassidy let her get it all out, and when the tears had subsided, she wiped Belle's face with a tissue and smiled.

Belle blew her nose. "Thanks, Cass."

"Anytime. Feel better?"

Belle lifted one thin shoulder in a halfhearted shrug. "A little, I guess."

"I don't know what to say to make you feel better about what you heard, Belle. You're right. Most grown-ups do have double standards. I'm not saying it's right, but I think it's their way of trying to protect us from the pitfalls they fell into as kids. All I can tell you for certain is that my uncle has loved your mother since they were kids."

Belle looked surprised. "He has?"

"They dated in secret when they were teenagers."

Belle rolled her eyes. "*Everybody* dated in secret."

"Yeah," Cassidy said with a smile. "It seems like it, doesn't it? I think it's because my uncle and my mom weren't considered good enough for the likes of Graysons and Hardistys."

"Another double standard," Belle said. "They tell me to treat everyone the same. No one is better than anyone else."

"Well, in their defense, I think it wasn't so much that your mom and Reed looked down on my mom and uncle as it was *their* parents did."

"Oh."

"Anyway, when Donovan went to jail, he broke off with your mom, so she wouldn't be—I don't know—hurt by all the bad things, I guess." Cassidy was putting the story together as she went along and pieces of the puzzle fell into place. "They went their separate ways, but he never forgot her, and he never found another woman he cared about as much."

"He never married anyone else?"

Cassidy shook her head. "He came back here for your mom as much as to start his own business."

''Really?''

''Really.''

Belle didn't say anything for several seconds. ''I should go to the police,'' she said with a sigh.

''Why?'' Cassidy asked, then remembered that in Belle's ''pretend'' story an innocent person was being blamed for something really bad.

''He couldn't have raped Lexie, Cassidy,'' Belle said. ''Because he was with my mom. I should tell Chief Landers, but I'm just so *mad* at them.''

''Well, I wouldn't worry about it right now. They haven't arrested Uncle Donovan, and I'm sure they'll find the person who did do it. I'm just as sure that if it came down to your being angry about something and doing the right thing, you'd do the right thing every time.''

Fifteen minutes later the adults had wrapped up their conversation. Belle's dad and Sophie were taking a walk to talk about the house, a new boy Cassidy had met had called her, and Donovan had left the house. On her own, feeling left out, Belle wandered out toward the greenhouses, curious to see how they were coming along and if Donovan had anything growing in them yet.

Empty. All of them. Feeling let down, she wandered around the side of the fifth greenhouse toward the huge pond that would supply the water for the plants. She was so entranced by the size of the pond and the gentle roll of tree-dotted hills around it that she didn't see Donovan until she'd almost run into him.

''Hey!''

She stopped a few feet from where he squatted, doing something to a scraggly, leafless rose bush. She plunged her hands into the pockets of her shorts. He looked terrible, she thought, so…tired. In spite of her anger, she felt a stirring of pity. "Hi."

"I'm sorry about last night," he said. "We should have been more discreet."

"You shouldn't have done it at all."

"You're right. And I have no excuse."

That pitiful look was getting to her. She hardened her heart and lifted her chin. "What do you plan to do about my mom?"

Donovan stood and stretched a kink out of his back. "Do?"

"Yeah. Are you just going to sleep with her until someone else comes along, or what?" Belle asked angrily.

"I want to marry her. I thought you knew that."

"Do I look like a mind reader?" Belle railed. "My mom has asked how I'd feel about it, but just because she's thought of marriage, doesn't mean you have. Adults treat kids like dadblamed mushrooms. You keep us in the dark and feed us—" she stopped "—well, you know."

"Yeah. Maybe we do. But since you asked, let me assure you that my intentions are honorable. I want us to be a family, Belle. Other than Cassidy and Sophie, I haven't had a family in a long time. How would you feel about that?"

Belle's heart broke a little more, yet she intuitively knew that Donovan wouldn't be happy if he knew she felt pity for him. And she wasn't ready to forgive him, or her mom, just yet.

"I'm not crazy about the idea. I'll think about it."

"Fair enough." He turned back to the plant, knelt on his knees and began to cut away another dead cane.

"Dad told me about Lexie."

Donovan grew very still. Belle sauntered closer, and he turned to look up at her.

"He told me you didn't do it, but I already knew that, 'cause you were with Mom." Her voice quavered a bit. "But even if you weren't, I know you couldn't have done it because you love living things too much to hurt one."

"Thank you, Belle. That may be the nicest thing anyone's ever said about me."

He wouldn't look at her, and his voice sounded funny. Sort of hoarse.

"What are you doing to that rose?" she asked. "It's dead."

"No, it isn't. It just has a lot of dead canes and it's lost its leaves for several reasons. See the new leaves coming out at the nodes?"

"It's ugly."

"It hasn't always been. It looks bad because it hasn't had any care in years. My mom used to have a lot of roses out here. The soil isn't very good for roses, but as long as she took care of them, they did okay. I guess she just got too busy to take care of them. But this is an antique rose, a hardy species, and somehow it's managed to survive droughts, pests and neglect for several years. When I saw it was struggling to stay alive, I thought I'd try to help. Sometimes a little TLC is all things need to thrive."

He offered her a wry smile. "Sort of like me and your mom."

"What do you mean?"

"Our feelings for each other weren't grounded in good soil, but in spite of all the years of neglect and the bad things that have happened, they've survived.

There are a lot of things, a lot of people against us, but I believe that with a little care and nurturing those new and tender sprouts of feelings we have can grow into something as beautiful as this rose will be. All we need is a chance.''

What he said made sense, but Belle saw the allegory in a different light. Donovan was the rosebush. The bad soil was his bad early life and his going to prison. But he was hardy, like the rose. Unlike the rose, he hadn't gotten ugly. He just hung in there, doing his best, trying his hardest and making the world more beautiful along the way.

She thought of the big smile on her mother's face when she'd come into the kitchen that morning, something she'd seen so seldom through the years. Always beautiful, at that moment Belle had thought her mom was gorgeous, in spite of her anger and disappointment.

"Belle! Come on! Time to go!"

The sound of Reed's voice drew her gaze from Donovan's. "I have to go."

Donovan nodded, and she turned and ran around the greenhouse toward her dad's car. She could hardly see for the sheen of tears glazing her eyes.

Donovan finished cutting away the old canes, his mind filled with thoughts of Lara and the need to see her, to hear her voice. But he wouldn't call. In his mind the whole ordeal with the police was like history repeating itself, a sort of test. The last time he'd been in trouble with the law, Lara had loved him enough to stand by him, even though he wouldn't let her. He wanted to see how much she loved him now.

Chapter Ten

After Donovan finished with the rose bush, he went inside. "Any calls?" he asked Cassidy. *Did Lara call?* "No."

Donovan didn't miss the covert glance that passed between Cassidy and Sophie. He hoped his pathetic disappointment didn't show. "I'm going to take a shower and go talk to Wes Grayson, see what my rights are."

While discussing the situation, Reed had agreed that he might not be the best person to represent Donovan, should that need arise. He'd recommended Wes, who held a record for winning criminal cases.

"I think that's smart," Sophie concurred. "Reed says Wes will leave no stone unturned at getting to the truth."

"You don't need to give me a sales pitch, Sis," Donovan said, picking a rose thorn from his finger and watching a small drop of blood gather in the small puncture. "I'm sold."

"Are you okay?" Sophie asked.

"I'm fine." He wasn't fine. His heart felt as if it had a rapier-size puncture wound and all the life was seeping out of him. He wanted Lara to call. Wanted her to tell him it was okay, that she would tell the police they'd been together while someone was forcing himself on Lexie Jamerson. But she hadn't called, and as more time passed and she didn't, Donovan feared she wouldn't.

He loved her and didn't doubt she still loved him. How deep that love went was another matter. A part of him feared Lara's job was more important to her than he was. Just as sadly, his freedom was more important to him than her job, so he understood all too well where she was coming from. If it came down to it, he'd tell them the truth, her job be hanged. He'd gone to jail once for a crime he hadn't committed. Call him selfish. Call him smarter. He had no intention of taking that route again. Ever. For anyone.

"Come on in," Wes Grayson said, taking Donovan's outstretched hand in a firm shake. "Reed told me to expect you."

"Thanks for seeing me," Donovan said, following Wes into the cabin's small living area and taking a seat on the leather sofa.

"No problem. I wasn't having a very good day with the paint, anyway." Wes dropped into an armchair and planted his elbows on denim-clad, paint-spattered thighs, leaning forward with sincere interest in his brown eyes. "You look good since the last time I saw you. How long has it been, anyway?"

"About eighteen years," Donovan said with a slow smile. "And thanks. You're holding up well yourself."

Wes patted his flat stomach. "We bachelors have to keep in shape, you know." The sarcasm in his voice mirrored the jaded expression in his eyes.

Donovan laughed. Like Reed, Wes had run with a different crowd, and Donovan hadn't known him well. As he remembered, Wes had been quiet but intense, occasionally exploding into unexplained anger, but he'd never been one to flaunt his wealth. More than once Donovan had entertained the idea that the anger was more directed toward himself than any person or thing and that Wes Grayson would have given anything to be someone other than who he was. He seemed happier, calmer, more content than he had in his youth. Maybe he'd finally found himself.

"So how have you been?" Wes asked.

"Fine. I finally got my degree in horticulture and I've been working and saving toward coming back here the past several years. No matter what happened, this is home."

Wes nodded. "You've caused quite a stir around town. I wish you'd heard Aunt Isabelle defend you the day the loan committee met to discuss your application." He laughed. "Discuss, hell. She told us we *would* give you the money, or she was pulling hers out of the bank."

"You're kidding," Donovan said, stunned. Though he knew Isabelle supported him, he had no idea to what length.

"Nope. And the thing is, she'd have done it, too. So now that you got the loan, how are things coming along?"

Donovan was still a little shocked by Isabelle's actions. "The greenhouses are on schedule, and I've picked up a fair amount of landscape business. It's getting too hot to do much outside right now. Come mid-July everyone just wants to keep what they have alive." He shrugged. "Everything was okay until this."

"To quote Aunt Isabelle, or the good book, 'This, too, shall pass.'"

"Yeah, but what's gonna be left when it does?"

Wes grinned. "Good point. Would you like something to drink? Since I gave up booze a few months ago, all I can offer you is cola or iced tea, but I have several exotic concoctions in my repertoire."

"Sweet tea?" Donovan asked.

"Is this the South?" Wes shot back. "Besides, a guy has to get his thrills some way."

"Sweet tea sounds great."

"I'll be right back," Wes said, rising.

Donovan watched him go, thinking that he liked Wes Grayson more than he had in the past. Liked him a lot, in fact. Clearly, there was no pussyfooting around with Wes. He was someone who said what he thought, told it like it was. How many men would volunteer the information that they were fighting a drinking problem? Donovan heard the clunk of ice falling into glasses, heard the refrigerator door's soft closure.

"So you and Lara were an item back in the stone age, huh?"

The question was called out from the direction of the kitchen. It caught Donovan completely off guard. He was still trying to come up with an answer a few seconds later, when Wes returned with a glass of tea in each hand. He handed one to Donovan and returned to his chair. He didn't seem angry, or surprised, only curious.

"Who told you?" Donovan asked.

"I overheard her and Aunt Isabelle talking the day we had lunch there. That one bit of information answered a lot of questions I'd had that Lara would never answer."

"It was a long time ago."

Wes raised his glass, smiled over the rim. "That isn't what I hear."

Donovan swore.

"You've forgotten how small towns are." He must have seen Donovan's distress, because he modified the statement with, "Actually, I heard it from Reed. He told me my sister is your alibi."

The tightness of Donovan's lips matched the tone of his voice. "Which I don't plan to say unless I absolutely have to."

"Why?"

"Truth?"

"Truth is always a good thing between an attorney and his potential client," Wes said. "I assume from what Reed says you think you need a lawyer."

So Wes was considering representing him, Donovan thought. "Okay. The truth is the lady is afraid she'll lose her job if the school board finds out she's seeing me. She wants to wait until after their annual review and be reasonably sure her position is secure before we go public."

Wes scratched at his lean cheek, which hadn't seen a razor in a couple of days. "She ought to know that's no guarantee. The only thing that bunch respects is bigger muscle. The only way to deal with them is to stand up and go at it nose to nose, the way Isabelle did the bank.''

''I said I'd give her the time,'' Donovan said, shrugging. ''We'll see what happens after that.''

''Have you talked to her about this newest wrinkle?''

''She hasn't called.''

The words spoke volumes to Wes. ''I'm sure she will.'' When Donovan didn't answer, he dropped all pretense of being a chatty, charming host. Concern as well as sincerity shone in his eyes. ''So let's talk about the facts.''

Donovan nodded.

''I know Bobby Landers. He's good at playing the crowd, and he likes to shake things up. When he heard what happened, he was smart enough to realize you'd be one of the first people some of the townsfolk would point a finger at, so he sent out one of his flunkies to question you. He's done two things.'' Wes held up two fingers to tick off the items. ''He's satisfied the local citizenry and he gives the impression of being on top of things. Actually, when the girl wakes up, she'll tell the authorities what happened, and that should be the end of it.''

''She isn't just a girl. She's Bud and Peggy Jamerson's daughter. I remember her when she was a baby.''

Though Donovan didn't realize it, the statement told Wes a lot about his potential client.

''Maybe I'm overreacting,'' Donovan said. ''But I don't mind telling you that when the police come around asking questions, I get a little nervous. I found out the hard way that life can throw you some curves. I want to be ready, just in case, and I heard you were really good,'' Donovan said.

Wes's lips twisted into a half smile. "Yeah. From my former brother-in-law."

"Reed's no fool."

"No," Wes said, "he isn't."

"If you're worried about money, I can pay—at least to a point."

Wes waved the comment aside. "If it comes down to it, you can do some landscaping around this place. It's been neglected for years."

He steepled his fingers together, placed the tips against his lips and regarded Donovan thoughtfully for several seconds. "Why not?" he said at last. "I've always been a champion of the underdog. No offense," he added quickly.

"None taken," Donovan replied. "So I do have an attorney, if the need arises?"

"Yes. If one of Bobby's men tries to question you again, call me and don't say a word until I get there."

Donovan nodded. He was familiar with the drill.

"Okay. Let's see where we are. They have no reason to suspect you, other than you have a record. If they keep coming around without any hard evidence I can scream violation of your civil rights and police harassment."

Donovan couldn't help being impressed.

"They haven't talked to the girl—Lexie—yet?" Wes asked.

"Not unless they have since earlier this morning."

Wes lifted his shoulders in a shrug. "Like I said, I think you're worrying unnecessarily. A statement from her should put an end to it."

"Should," Donovan said. "I just want to be ready for the unexpected."

* * *

Donovan went home from Wes's and changed his clothes. Then he went out to check on Jett's progress on the greenhouse—which was slow, due to his working alone and his hangover. Jett blamed Cassidy for the whole thing. They'd dated a few times when she'd first come to Lewiston, but Jett was three years older than Cass, and since she and Sophie had come back, she'd refused to go out with him. He wouldn't say anything to Donovan about her reasons, but Donovan had a pretty good idea what they were. Cass's hormones were waging war with her common sense, and so far her common sense was holding its own.

"Maybe it's the age thing," he told Jett, trying to make light of what might be a serious situation. "She's getting ready to start school here, and you're already out. While it's cool to have an older boyfriend, sometimes it makes you feel like an outsider at school. But be clear on one thing, Jett. Your getting loaded is not Cassidy's fault. Ultimately we're all responsible for our behavior. We all make the choice about how we're going to handle the problems that crop up."

"You sound like my mom."

"Good. We've both lived a lot more life than you have, and we've learned a few things. I don't have all the answers, but there's one thing I can promise you. If you turn to drinking every time things don't go as planned, you'll wind up a nobody going nowhere."

Jett nodded. "I know. It was stupid, and I swear I won't do it again. I've had a few too many a time or two, but I was stinking drunk last night, and if today is what it's like getting over it, it isn't worth it."

"Good," Donovan said, hoping the younger man meant what he said.

He and Jett were stretching some plastic when Cassidy came out onto the front porch with the cordless phone and yelled, ''Uncle Donovan! It's for you!''

Donovan handed Jett the staple gun and headed back toward the house, wondering why the call couldn't have come a few minutes earlier, while he was inside. He took the phone from Cassidy and barked ''Hello!'' into the mouthpiece.

''Donovan?''

Lara. Why hadn't Cassidy told him? At the sound of her voice, the tension and frustration binding him eased. His anger didn't. ''I didn't expect you to call.''

He heard her sudden intake of air. ''That isn't fair,'' she said softly.

''Life isn't fair, babe, or haven't you heard?'' There was a bite to the question.

''Wes doesn't seem to think you have anything to worry about.''

Donovan's senses went on alert. He recalled Wes saying flatly that Lara *would* call. ''You've talked to him?''

''Yes.''

''Did he tell you to call?''

The pause on the other end of the line was all the answer he needed. Donovan closed his eyes against a sudden, unbearable pain. Why couldn't she love him more? Why had God given him a half loaf when it wasn't nearly enough? ''I don't think we have anything more to say to each other.''

''Wait!''

''What?''

''If it comes down to it, and I have to tell them to clear your name, I will.''

If it comes down to it. She would tell them the truth

to save him from jail, but only if she had to.

"Goodbye, Lara," he said and hung up.

It was midafternoon when Jimmy French drove out to Donovan's with the police chief. Donovan saw the car coming down the lane and went into the house to call Wes. He said he'd be right over. By the time Donovan hung up, the two Lewiston policemen were getting out of the car.

He sauntered out onto the porch and stood regarding them, his legs splayed, his fingertips tucked into the front pockets of his jeans. "Good afternoon, gentlemen," he said with far more composure than he felt. "Would you like to sit down?"

"This isn't a social call, Delaney," Bobby Landers snapped, climbing the short flight of steps. "We'd like you to come down to the station to answer some questions about the Lexie Jamerson case."

"I told you I had nothing to do with that," Donovan said, clinging to his self-control like a suction cup to a piece of glass.

"We have some new evidence that says otherwise," Bobby said.

Donovan hoped his surprise didn't show. What could they possibly have to connect him to a seventeen-year-old girl he hadn't seen since she was an infant? "Have you questioned Lexie?"

"Whoa, Delaney!" the police chief said. "You've got this all wrong. You don't ask the questions, we do. Now, are you coming peacefully, or do we have to cuff you?"

"I'll come quietly, but do you mind waiting for my attorney to arrive?"

"Attorney?" Bobby gave Jimmy a half smile and

drawled, "You seem awfully prepared for an innocent man."

"I know how a lot of police forces try to pin every crime they can on ex-cons. I'm just protecting my rights."

Bobby raised his chin to a belligerent angle. "We don't operate that way."

"Good. Then we neither have anything to worry about, do we?" He glanced at his watch. "Wes should be here any minute."

"Wes?" Bobby shot Jimmy a look of surprise. When he spoke, his voice was grim, angry. "Grayson is your attorney?"

Wondering what Bobby had against Wes, Donovan nodded. "Yep."

As if the discussion had conjured him up, Wes's antique roadster convertible came barreling down the lane in a cloud of dust that resembled magicians' smoke. Wes must have broken every speed limit between the cabin and his place, Donovan thought. As the trio watched, the car skidded to a stop, Wes opened the door, unfolded his lean, elegant frame and stepped out. He was wearing a confident smile and the paint-smeared clothes he'd had on earlier.

"Hello, Bobby. Jimmy. Sorry I'm late."

Jimmy spoke. Bobby didn't.

"Did I miss anything?"

"Not really," Donovan said. "They say they have new evidence that places me at the scene. The party was about to move downtown."

Wes turned a bland gaze to the police chief. "My client has an alibi."

"So he says," Bobby concurred, biting out the

words in a clear effort to hold back his anger. "But so far we haven't heard it."

Wes pinned Bobby with a hard glare. "Are you arresting him?"

Clearly hoping to defuse the situation, Jimmy jumped in. "We just want to ask him a few more questions, Wes, and we'd like to make sure we do this by the book."

"That's why I'm here," Wes said. "So why are we waiting? Let's go."

The Lewiston grapevine was in fine working order. The ink had barely dried from entering the new evidence into the log than the officer in charge told another one, who promptly called another on his radio. Calvin Turner, a paraplegic who spent much of his day listening to his police scanner for juicy tidbits, heard the news and called his mother. She called two friends who called two more. Reed got the information approximately thirty minutes later and called Lara to tell her the bad news.

The interrogation room was small, but because the city had funded some repairs and renovations to city hall and the adjoining jail, there was nothing dirty and depressing about it. The upper portion of the walls were painted off-white and the wainscot was a chocolate-brown. There was a nice oak table that, so far showed minimal signs of defacement, and the straight-back chairs, while by no means comfortable, were also new.

"So what's the new evidence?" Wes asked when they were all settled and all the formalities had been tended to.

"We found an article of clothing at the scene that we believe belongs to Delaney," Bobby said.

"What piece of clothing?" Wes asked.

"A T-shirt with the Delaney logo."

"No way!" Donovan said.

"That's pretty weak, Bobby," Wes said. "There are probably dozens of people in town who own those T-shirts."

"Yeah, but so does Delaney."

Wes rolled his eyes and turned to Donovan. "He knows it isn't much, or he'd go ahead and arrest you. What size T-shirt do you wear?"

"Extra large," Donovan said.

Wes turned to the police chief. "What size is the shirt you found?"

"Large," Bobby said grudgingly.

Wes rose. "I rest my case. Let's get out of here."

"Now just wait a damn minute, Grayson!" Bobby said loudly. "Who's running this interrogation?"

"There is no interrogation, Bobby. That is not my client's shirt."

"We don't know that for sure. Just because he might not have been wearing it, it could still be his. He might have had it in his truck."

"And maybe you're barking up the wrong tree."

If looks could kill, Wes Grayson would be long gone, Donovan thought, wondering again at the enmity between the two men.

"You have no real evidence against him, Bobby. The way I see it, the actions of this office are borderline harassment. Book him or let him go."

Bobby Landers looked ready to explode. The air in the room was thick with pressure. A smiling young policeman stuck his head in the door. He picked up on the stress and the brilliance of the smile dimmed.

"What is it?" Bobby snapped.

The young officer's gaze moved from one person to another, finally landing on Bobby, who had risen and was moving toward the door, Jimmy two steps behind him. "Uh, a couple of things. The hospital called. The Jamerson girl is awake. We got a couple of calls. One from the high school principal—"

The rest of the statement was cut off by the closing of the door as Bobby and Jimmy took the conversation outside the room. Wes smiled. Donovan felt an overwhelming sense of relief. Lara had come through after all.

Bobby stuck his head back inside and looked at Wes, palpable hostility radiating from him. "You know I can hold him for twenty-four hours without charging him, so you two wait here until I get back." He closed the door before Wes could respond.

Wes shrugged. Donovan closed his eyes. It was almost over. Lara had called. She would tell the police he was with her during the time the rape had taken place, and Lexie would confirm that he had nothing to do with it. He'd soon have his life back.

Lara hung up the phone and turned, gasping in surprise when she saw Belle standing across the room. She tried to summon a smile. "I just called the police."

"I heard you."

"I told them they should talk to Darren Potect, Lexie's ex-boyfriend. I thought telling them that he's caused her a lot of trouble in the past might convince them they should be looking at someone besides Donovan.''

"Why didn't you just tell the police he couldn't have done it because he was here with you? In your bedroom? You've always told me to tell the truth.''

Lara flinched at the animosity in Belle's voice and the disappointment in her eyes. A huge rush of guilty sorrow washed through her. "It's…complicated, honey,'' she said. "You wouldn't understand.''

Belle's face turned red. "Stop treating me like a baby!'' she cried. "I'm going to be thirteen in a few months, and I understand more than you think. Maybe more than you do.''

Lara took a step toward her, an entreating hand outstretched. "Belle—''

Belle took a step back, and Lara let her hand fall to her side.

"I understand that this is about a lot more than what people will say if they find out about you and Donovan.'' Seeing the question in Lara's eyes, she said, "Cassidy and I talked. I know you're worried about your job, but that isn't the important thing, Mom. It's just a stupid job! You should be worried about Donovan.'' Tears started in her eyes, and she blinked them back. "Donovan is…special. He's been through a lot, and he's still a good person. He doesn't deserve people thinking bad things about him.''

Lara felt her own eyes begin to burn. She scoured her mind for something to say to redeem herself in her daughter's eyes and feared there was nothing.

"You're always saying that relationships require sacrifices. He loves you, Mom, and he isn't saying anything to the police about being here because he wants to protect you. If you really loved him, wouldn't you do the same thing? Wouldn't you want to do whatever it took to protect him? I would.''

When Lara made no immediate answer, Belle gave a little cry of anger and stormed from the room. Lara started to call her back, but there was nothing to say. There was no argument to Belle's logic. How could there be when the sentiments and words coming from her were Lara's own, when her observations about Donovan were the same observations Lara herself had made years before? For the thousandth time, she wondered how her daughter had become so wise.

The phone rang, startling her from her troubled thoughts. She picked up the phone and pushed the on button. ''Hello.''

''Thank you, thank you, thank you!'' Wes said, his pleasure apparent.

Lara's heart leaped. Had the police turned Donovan loose? ''For what?''

''For calling and telling the police Donovan was with you.''

''I didn't.''

''They've gone to the hospital now to talk to…'' Wes's voice trailed away as her denial registered.

''What do you mean you didn't? I heard them say you called.''

That nagging guilt, spurred by Belle's anger and disappointment, deepened. Lara would have rather cut off her pinkie than admit the truth. She gave a hearty sigh. ''I called, but I didn't tell them he was here. I started thinking about all the trouble Darren Poteet has given Lexie since they broke up. He's been like *stalking* her, and I thought—''

''I can't believe you, Lara,'' Wes said, clearly bewildered. ''That's important stuff, and it should have been told, but for the love of God, why didn't you tell them Donovan was with you? Never mind. Don't answer that.''

''Wes...''

''I have to go, Lara,'' Wes said in his coldest, most lawyerish-sounding voice. ''Somehow I have to tell my client that the woman he loves still hasn't come through for him. Of course, I'm sure Lexie's statement will clear him, but I really think he'd rather it have been you.''

Lara heard the click as her brother hung up, and turned her own phone off. What had she been thinking? Wes and Belle were right. The whole thing wasn't about whether or not Donovan was innocent or guilty. It never had been. It wasn't about Lexie Jamerson's statement setting him free or Darren Poteet's possible guilt. It was about how much she loved Donovan. How much she believed in him.

Belle was right, too. It was only a stupid job, and Donovan was special. Very special. She'd longed for a chance to turn back time and somehow make things come out right, knowing that could never happen. When she and Reed split up, she'd wished for a second chance to find happiness, and God had sent Donovan back to Lewiston. Miraculously he still loved her. Foolishly she'd taken that love, used it for her own selfish pleasure and then thrown it back in his face when he needed her support the most.

Lara buried her face in her hands and let the tears flow, drowning in remorse and shame. Sure, she'd needed her principal's position to boost her self-esteem after her marriage had broken up, but when had a job become more important to her than people? How could she have been so selfish? So cruel? Was there a way to make it up to Donovan? Would he even care that she did? Or had she hurt him so badly that whatever attempt she made to make things right wouldn't even matter?

After a bout of self-castigation and severe crying, Lara went upstairs to tell Belle she was going to the police station to tell them the truth, but her daughter was nowhere to be found.

Lara knew better than to panic. Familiar with her Belle's habits, she figured she was either at her friend's house, telling her what a terrible person her mother was, or at Isabelle's being petted and pampered, Isabelle's treatment of choice for anger and hurt feelings. A phone call assured her that Belle was indeed with Isabelle, that she was fine. That worry alleviated, Lara gathered her courage and her car keys and started for the door. She was pulling the door shut when the phone rang. She debated on whether or not to answer and decided that it might be someone with news of Donovan.

It was Rowland Hardisty.

"I can't talk, Rowland," she said, her heart beating fast. "I'm on my way out." No way she was telling him where she was going. No sense waving a red flag in his face.

"I just wanted to warn you that you're playing with fire."

"I don't know what you mean."

"Of course you do. I'm talking about your...what shall we call it? Your involvement with Donovan Delaney. And don't try to deny it. Your lies the other day at Lagniappe's didn't fool me."

"Whether or not I'm involved with Donovan is

none of your business. I'm not married to Reed anymore.''

"No but you are still the mother of my granddaughter, and I won't have her exposed to the likes of Delaney on a regular basis. My son may have taken leave of his senses by deciding to marry that woman, but I'll be damned if I'll stand for two Delaneys infiltrating my family.''

"First, I'm not part of your family, and second, I have no idea what may happen between me and Donovan. What I do know is that whatever happens, there's nothing you can do about it.''

"Maybe you're right. I may not have a say in what you do with your personal life, but I do have considerable influence over the school board.''

There it was. The thing she'd been so worried about. Somehow it didn't seem nearly as terrible as she'd imagined. Or maybe it was that it didn't matter anymore. "You do what you have to do, Rowland,'' she said. "Now if you'll excuse me, I really have to go.''

Lara hung up before he could reply, and wasted no time driving across town to the police station. She approached the dispatcher's desk with determined trepidation. The young man behind the desk looked familiar. Luke Harrison, Lara thought, putting a name to the face she remembered from the high school no more than four years ago.

"Hello, Ms. Hardisty,'' he said smiling at her. "I told the chief you called. Is there something else I can do for you?''

"I'd like to speak to Bobby, please,'' Lara said. "I have some other information about the rape that's very important.''

Luke gave her a strange look, clearly curious about

what information she might possess about a rape case. "He isn't here right now. He's gone to the hospital to take the Jamerson girl's statement. Would you like to talk to someone else?"

Disappointment spread through Lara, nibbling away at her resolve. "No," she said. "I really need to talk to Bobby." She turned to go.

"You're welcome to wait here, if you like," Luke told her.

"Yes," she said, grabbing at the offer gratefully. "I'd like that." She was afraid that if she left, she might not find the courage to come back.

Luke led her to a small, musty-smelling room that looked as if it got minimal use.

"Would you like a cup of coffee while you wait, Ms. Hardisty?" he asked.

"That would be nice," she said, touched by his thoughtfulness.

He returned a few minutes later with a foam cup of something that bore a greater resemblance to oil-well sludge than a liquid beverage, a couple of sugar and creamer packets.

"The chief should be back soon." He set the cup on the dusty desk, said "Enjoy" and left her alone in the room.

Lara took one whiff of the coffee and shuddered. No amount of sugar and creamer could help that stuff. She left it sitting and wandered around the small room, taking stock of its meager amenities—a cheap desk with a dirty ashtray, a swivel chair and a vinyl sofa with a couple of hunting magazines scattered on top. Rumor had it that Bobby liked his afternoon naps.

She paced for a while, then, with nothing else to do, she picked up one of the hunting magazines and sat down on the sofa, realizing she was exhausted. She'd slept fitfully the day before, and then Donovan had paid her that impromptu visit…. She flipped open to the first article and started to read, but not even the promise of how to nab a trophy buck could keep her awake. She was asleep within minutes of sitting down.

Out at the station's front desk, a new shift came on. Not since Donovan was arrested for shooting his father had any news so rocked the town, and in the excitement of relating the information about the recent questioning, Luke Harrison completely forgot to tell his replacement that Lara Hardisty was waiting in an unused office to talk to the chief.

Chapter Eleven

The hour since Bobby had gone seemed like four times that. Donovan stared unseeingly at a calendar on the wall for several seconds and paced the small room, unable to banish the feeling that the walls were closing in on him, unable to stop the pain that throbbed through him with every beat of his heart. His newly acquired attorney was nothing if not truthful, and he'd come back from making the thank-you call to Lara with the truth: Lara still hadn't told the police they were together the night before.

Donovan glanced at Wes, slouched in a chair at the table. His hands were folded over his stomach, and his eyes were closed, the picture of unconcern except for the tightness around his mouth. He was furious with his sister, but strangely, Donovan wasn't angry anymore. There was no room for anger inside him. He was too full of disappointment.

He checked the time again. What was taking Bobby so long? "What's with you and Bobby Landers?" Donovan said, weary of the silence and curious about the animosity between the two men.

Wes opened one eye. A ghost of a smile played at the corners of his mouth. "Couple of things, actually. He was accused of sexual harassment by a female co-worker several years ago, and I represented her. Unfortunately, Lewiston was—still is—in the grip of the good-ol'-boys' mentality, and the jury took the approach that boys will be boys. Even though he beat the charge, he's never forgiven me for siding against him. I also dated his ex-wife a couple of years ago, and he's still carrying a torch for her, though I can't imagine why. She was fairly entertaining in bed, but outside of that, she's a nagging witch."

Donovan couldn't help smiling. The sound of approaching footsteps terminated the smile. The doorknob turned, and the police chief and Jimmy French pushed through.

The exultant expression on Bobby's face was hard to miss. He tossed Wes a triumphant glance and turned to Donovan. "Donovan Delaney, you're under arrest for the rape of Lexie Jamerson."

Donovan felt as if all the air had been sucked from the room, which took a sharp dip. He grabbed the back of a nearby chair to support himself.

Wes exploded from his chair. "On what grounds?"

"The statement we just took from the victim," Bobby said. "And the shirt found at the scene."

"Did she actually say the man who raped her was Donovan?"

"No. She said she was sneaked up on and rushed from the side. Her assailant threw something over her face, so she couldn't see who it was, but she did get a glimpse of his shirt. She definitely remembers seeing the Delaney logo.''

"That's pretty thin," Wes said. "Especially since we've already established that the shirt isn't Donovan's size."

"Yeah, well, people wear the wrong size all the time for a lot of reasons." He gave Donovan a pointed look. "Since he hasn't come up with an alibi for that night, he had means and opportunity."

"What about motive?" Wes asked.

Bobby shrugged. "He was in prison a long time."

"And he's been out a long time. Besides, any lawman worth his salt knows rape isn't about sex. It's about anger and power."

"So maybe he's come back to town wanting to prove something to everyone."

"And maybe you're making a really big mistake." Bobby shrugged, and Wes pointed his finger at the police chief. "This one is going to come back and bite you on the butt."

"Tell it to the judge," Bobby said, opening the door and making a sweeping gesture. He looked at Donovan with another of those self-satisfied smirks. "You have the right to remain—"

Donovan heard the familiar words of the Miranda without really listening. All he could think of was that history really did repeat itself.

Word of Donovan's arrest hit the street just moments after Bobby Landers ushered him to a holding cell. The dispatcher, father of two teenage girls, called his wife to tell her they'd arrested Donovan Delaney, not to worry about the girls anymore. Then he called

the sheriff's department and told them of the arrest.
That dispatcher called Sheriff Micah Lawrence, who
was at his granddaughter's birthday party, to spread
the news.

Promising Donovan he wouldn't have to spend the
night in jail, Wes pulled some strings and managed to
get a bail hearing with a judge in two hours. Bobby
announced that he'd be back in time for the hearing,
and, as he was wont to do when there was a lull around
the station, went home to catch a nap.

Wes watched Bobby go and decided to tell Lara it
was time to come forward with her corroboration of
Donovan's alibi. He called her, but no one was at
home. He had no idea she was sitting in a small room
down the hall, waiting to tell the police chief the truth
about Donovan's whereabouts the night before. She
had no idea he'd already been arrested.

Unable to reach his sister, Wes called Reed, who
called Isabelle. Then he drove out to tell Sophie and
Cassidy in person. As he expected, Sophie took it hard,
breaking into hysterical sobbing.

In tears herself, Cassidy went into her bedroom and
called Jett, the only person she felt she could talk to,
the only person in town other than Belle she could call
a friend. She told Jett everything she knew: about the
authorities finding the Delaney Landscape T-shirt at
the scene and what Lexie had said about seeing it on
her assailant. Jett listened, swore and said he'd be over
as soon as he ran an errand. He told his mom—who
called her two sisters—what was going on and left his
house slinging gravel and churning dust.

Wes mulled things over, thinking that there must be
something he could do to shed some new light on the
situation. Remembering Lara's statement about Darren

Poteet, Wes left the station and headed for the hospital to get the Jamersons' take on their daughter's relationship with her ex-boyfriend. Somehow, he had to uncover something to turn the afternoon's events around.

Belle was at Isabelle's when her dad called with news of Donovan's arrest. She promptly burst into tears. She'd already told Aunt Isabelle about hearing her mother and Donovan in her mom's bedroom the night of the rape and about her mother's reluctance to say anything to the authorities because of her job. She'd told Isabelle she didn't want Donovan to go to prison again.

Isabelle comforted her with cookies and lemonade and a walk through the garden as they discussed the situation.

"Your mother is a good person, Belle. I know she's disappointed you by telling you to do one thing and doing something else, but you must remember, child, that none of us is perfect. Oftentimes we do things we don't plan to do, and sometimes we have hard choices to make. Like your mother and Donovan. Weighing the wrongness against her feelings for him had to be a difficult decision. The same with her job and telling the authorities about Donovan being with her. I'm not saying either thing is right, I'm just trying to make you see that sometimes the right choices are hard choices. But she'll do the proper thing in the end. She always has."

"But what if she doesn't?" Belle wailed.

"What do you think you should do? What can you do?"

"I could go to the police myself, and tell them what I know, but then what if Mom does lose her job?"

Isabelle's eyes held a world of tenderness. She brushed back a wayward strand of Belle's hair with fingers gnarled by arthritis. "See?" she said with a gentle smile. "That's exactly what I'm talking about. A hard decision. But maybe I can help."

"How?"

"You do what you think you should do and don't worry about your mother's job. I'm on the school board, you know, and I think I can persuade the others to see things my way."

"Really?" Belle asked, her face glowing.

"Oh, I think so," Isabelle said. She stood and held out her hand to Belle. "Let's go find Rodney. He can drive you to the police station. It's too hot out to ride your bicycle so far."

When the gleaming aged Bentley pulled to the curb in front of the police station, Ted Kemp, who'd taken over the manning of the dispatcher's desk from Luke Harrison, glanced up from the *Babes* magazine he was looking at. He recognized the Bentley as Isabelle Duncan's and wondered what would bring her down to the station. To his surprise, it wasn't Isabelle who got out of the car, but a girl about twelve years old. He shoved the magazine into a drawer. The girl spoke to the driver, shook her head and waved him away. She looked so much like the old lady, Ted had to smile. He watched as the girl—Reed Hardisty's kid if looks had anything to do with it—squared her shoulders and marched through the front doors and straight to the desk, meeting his curious gaze with a look of determination not often seen on a kid her age.

"I need to talk to someone about Lexie Jamerson's

rape,'' she said in a tone that held a surprising ring of authority.

By the time Wes reached the hospital, he was in rare fighting form. He had no intention of taking Donovan's arrest lying down, so to speak. Lara's information about Lexie and Darren's past trouble was a good lead, and if Bobby was so stupid as to ignore it in his eagerness to put Donovan behind bars, Wes would check it out himself.

The first person he saw when he stepped off the elevator was Rowland Hardisty. The town's renowned surgeon was standing near the nurses' station, writing on a chart. Wes and Reed had been friends since their diaper days, and their fathers had been friends since theirs, so Wes had grown up in Rowland's presence. He'd never liked Reed's dad.

A perfectionist and a controller by nature, Rowland had meddled too much in his son's life, unlike Wes's own dad, who'd never cared enough to meddle. It was a great commentary on Celeste Hardisty's influence that Reed had turned out as well as he had. As it was, Wes never ran into Rowland—who made no secret of the fact that he thought Wes was a loser and a disappointment to his father's memory—without feeling he was being measured and coming up short.

Fighting that feeling now, he said, ''Hello, Rowland.''

He saw the older man's lips thin in disapproval. It chapped Rowland that since the age of twenty-one Wes had taken to calling him by his first name instead of calling him ''Mr. Hardisty'' and ''Sir.''

''Weston,'' Rowland said with a slight nod. ''What are you doing here?''

Wes rubbed a palm down his whisker-stubbled cheek. "I'm representing Donovan Delaney, and I thought I'd come have a talk with the Jamersons."

Rowland's smile, as he gave Wes's attire the once-over, gave the word *condescending* a whole new meaning. "You're representing him? I thought you preferred to spend your days with a paintbrush and a bottle, instead of pulling your weight at the office."

The comment was low, even for Rowland. But Wes had never been a slouch in the cut-down department himself. He exhaled slowly and counted to ten. "Rude, Rowland. Very rude. Haven't you heard? I did a stint at Betty Ford. While I was there I learned that the first step to overcoming an addiction is recognizing that you have a problem. But I guess there isn't much hope for you, because even if you did acknowledge you had one, I'm not aware of any rehab programs for narcissism."

Rowland's fingers tightened on the chart. From years of experience, Wes knew the older man would take a new tack. He wasn't the kind to engage in an ongoing battle. His style was to hit and run.

"I thought Bobby already had Delaney in custody."

"They do, but unlike Bobby, I'm a thorough guy. There's at least one loose end that needs some checking out."

"Why on earth do you care what happens to Donovan Delaney?" Rowland asked. "I'd think you'd be happy that he was going up the river again."

"What do you mean?"

"I saw him with Lara at Lagniappe a while back," Rowland said with a slight shrug. "They pretended they weren't together, but it was clear that they were. You know, his arrest might be a blessing in disguise for her. If the school board had gotten wind that she was involved with Delaney, it wouldn't have been good.''

Evidently Lara's concern over her job was real. "And I'm sure you'd have told them sooner or later.''

"It may have escaped your notice, Weston, but as a member of the school board, I have a responsibility to the children of the community.''

Wes's smile was as twisted as Rowland's logic. "The man paid his debt to society. He isn't a threat.''

"Tell that to Lexie Jamerson.''

"She didn't say he did it. All she saw was a shirt. Hell,'' Wes said, "I have one of those shirts. Besides, it's hard for me to believe that a man who went to prison to protect a teenage girl could be guilty of something like this.''

"Why are you defending him?'' Rowland asked. "I wouldn't think you'd be too pleased that your sister is interested in him.''

"It's her life, and to tell the truth, I always liked the guy.''

"Well, he isn't the kind of man I want hanging around my granddaughter, though I suppose that's moot, now, with him headed to Pine Bluff.''

"It ain't over till the fat lady sings,'' Wes said. "Look, as much as I've enjoyed our little chat, I really have to run.''

Without waiting for Rowland's reply, Wes turned and started toward the waiting room at the end of the corridor, offering an automatic smile at the blond nurse headed his way. If he'd stopped the pretty LPN and had her check his blood pressure, it would have been sky-high. As usual, when he got angry or upset, he felt the need for a drink. He stopped at a small room that

held various vending machines, shoved some change
into the slot and punched the button for a cola.

After taking several healthy swallows, Wes felt better, as much from being away from Rowland as from
the jolt of caffeine. Five minutes later he finished the
cola, tossed the can into the trash and headed toward
the waiting room.

For the moment the Jamersons had passed the crying, crazy-with-grief phase and the anger phase. They
were both numb with exhaustion and sick with worry.

Bud Jamerson recognized him, and they shook
hands. They knew about Donovan's arrest, and when
Wes told them he was representing Donovan and
wanted to ask them a few questions, they both agreed.
Bud said exactly what Wes maintained, that dozens of
people in town owned Delaney Landscape T-shirts. He
did, in fact. Besides, he'd known Donovan a long time
and didn't believe he was capable of what he was accused of.

"My sister tells me that Lexie has had some trouble
with Darren Poteet," Wes said.

Bud nodded. "Not *some* trouble. Lots of trouble. He
calls all hours of the night. He goes to her job and
hangs around outside waiting for her to come out, and
he got pretty violent with her at the school a few weeks
ago. I'm sure Ms. Hardisty can tell you all about it."

"So he has shown signs of violence?" Wes asked.

"Definitely," Bud said.

"He caused a big scene at a party she went to a few
nights ago with a new boyfriend. It had gotten to the
place she was afraid to go anywhere he might show
up, afraid of what he might do," Peggy Jamerson offered. Her eyes were troubled. "She told him it was

over months ago, but it's like he's obsessed with her, like he can't bear to let her go.''

"Can you tell me where Darren lives?" Wes asked.

"Sure. Out on Highway 82 East, the yellow frame house on the left at the edge of town.''

"You think he did this, don't you?" Peggy asked.

"I'm not a psychologist or a cop," Wes said, "but I'm almost certain of it.''

Wes found the Poteet house with no trouble and drove past it to check things out. The house was medium size and well maintained. A swing set sat in the backyard, along with a doghouse and a shed with a lean-to attached. An army-green four-wheeler and a bright-orange riding lawn mower sat beneath the lean-to. There were no vehicles in the driveway, but that didn't mean no one was at home.

He pulled into the driveway and went to the front door. There was no doorbell, so Wes knocked and waited. Knocked again. Still no answer. He went to the back door and tried again, still getting no response. If there was someone inside, it would take the police to get them out. He had no choice but to go back to the station, try to get Donovan out on bail and start trying to prove his innocence. If he had the Jamersons talk to Bobby about Darren, maybe the chief would at least have someone look into the possibility that he'd laid the guilt on the wrong man.

Jett Robbins wasn't sure when he'd been so upset, both by Cassidy's tears, something that had made men nervous and inadequate feeling since God created the species, or because an innocent man had been arrested. Jett had been leery of going to work for Donovan when his uncle, who had done the remodeling on the Delaney house, had suggested it. Jett had never been around anyone who'd been to jail before, but his uncle had vouched for Donovan, claiming that he'd done the world a favor.

Jett's interview had consisted of an informal talk over Cokes and Twinkies. After asking Jett about himself, Donovan had given Jett the *Reader's Digest* version of what had happened and told him if he felt uncomfortable working for him, he understood. Jett figured anyone who consumed as much junk food as he himself did couldn't be all bad. Within the day, Donovan had banished whatever concerns Jett might have had with his slow smile, his dry sense of humor and his patience with Jett's lack of skill.

Jett had become pretty good buds with his employer the past couple of months, and he liked working for Donovan. There was no way he was going to let him take the fall for something he hadn't done. Jett knew Darren Poteet was the person who'd hurt Lexie, and he also knew how the Delaney Landscape T-shirt had come to be in Darren's possession.

The day before, Jett had seen Darren's old truck sitting on the shoulder of the road, with the hood up. Though he was no particular fan of Darren's, Jett had stopped to see if he could help, having been stranded before himself. Darren had been under the vehicle, cursing.

"Need some help?"

Darren scooted out from under the truck, a disgusted look on his face. "Naw," he said, getting to his feet. "The engine's blown oil all over. It won't even register on the dipstick. I'll have to have it towed in."

"Can I drop you off somewhere, then?" Jett asked.

"Yeah," Darren said, already heading toward the passenger side of the truck. "That'd be great. I was headed over to Tommy Medrano's. We were gonna go catch a movie."

"Landry Lane?" Jett asked as they climbed into the truck.

"Yeah."

Jett cast a glance at Darren. "I hate to tell you but there's oil all over the back of your shirt."

Darren swore and tugged the shirt over his head. "Did it get on your seats?"

"I don't think so." Jett reached under his seat and pulled out the extra T-shirt he kept in the truck for emergencies. "Here," he'd said, thrusting it at Darren. "You can borrow this one. It's okay for the movies, and it'll save you having to go home and get another one."

"Hey, thanks, man," Darren had said as he unfolded the shirt.

Now, standing at the Poteet's front door, waiting to see if anyone answered his knock, Jett's blood boiled. He knocked again. When there was no answer, he left the porch and started for his truck.

Then he heard the door open and turned. Darren stood in the doorway, his hair rumpled and a sleepy smile on his face. "Hey, Jett. Sorry it took so long for me to come to the door, but I was asleep and couldn't seem to get my eyes open. Did you stop by earlier?"

"No," Jett said, shaking his head and making note of four long scratches on Darren's cheek and neck.

"I thought I heard someone knocking a while ago, but I just couldn't get up." Darren scraped back his too-long hair with one hand and pushed through the screen door with the other, crossing the porch and joining Jett on the lawn.

"It wasn't me." Jett whistled. "Those are some kind of nasty-looking scratches. What happened?"

Darren lifted a hand to his cheek. "Uh…Tommy and I were scoutin' out the squirrel woods." A troubled expression entered his eyes. "I really appreciate your help the other day. Was there something I could do for you?"

"Naw. I was just out this way, and I thought I'd stop by and see what was wrong with your truck." The lie tripped easily from Jett's tongue.

"I'm not sure what's wrong, but it's in the shop even as we speak," Darren told him, forcing a smile.

"Oh. And I was wondering if I could pick up my T-shirt. Mr. Delaney likes me to wear the shirts when I'm on the job. Sort of advertising, you know?"

"Uh…gee, I'll bet it's in the wash. If you like, I'll go check."

"If you don't mind," Jett said.

As Darren reached the porch steps, Jett said, "Man, it was terrible about Lexie, wasn't it?"

Darren turned. His face was a study in nonchalance, but it had lost all its color. "What about her?"

"You didn't hear?" Jett said, pretending shock. "She was raped last night."

"No kidding?"

"No. I'm surprised you didn't know." When Darren flinched, Jett added. "I mean, it's all over town. Since you two used to be an item, I'm surprised no one called you."

"No. No one." Darren's voice was hushed. He was giving a reasonable impersonation of an innocent man, Jett thought, but he was trying so hard to act normal, he wasn't showing nearly enough emotion for some-one whose ex-girlfriend had been raped. "Do they have any idea who did it?"

Jett decided not to tell Darren about Donovan's ar-rest. "Whoever did it put something over Lexie's face. They're trying to pin the thing on Mr. Delaney, be-cause he has a record and because Lexie said whoever did it was wearing a Delaney Landscape T-shirt."

The words were no sooner out of Jett's mouth than Darren turned and bolted up the steps. Jett was on him in three long strides, spinning him around and smack-ing his fist into Darren's face. He hit the porch with a thud, and Jett was on him in a flash, fist raised.

"Don't!" Darren cried, tears in his eyes. "Don't."

Jett hauled Darren to his feet. "Come on. I'm taking you to have a little talk with Bobby Landers."

Micah Lawrence was a troubled man. He'd received the information about Donovan's arrest while he was at his granddaughter's birthday party. The idea that Donovan could be responsible for such an outrage was unthinkable, especially since Micah knew about the sacrifice Donovan had made for his sister. There was no way a man who possessed that much honor could do anything so terrible. Besides, Micah knew full well that Donovan had been at Lara Hardisty's at the time the rape was committed. Micah had seen Donovan's Explorer in the drive as he'd left his own secret assig-nation with the widow Meriweather.

Now he was stuck between the proverbial rock and hard place: as a law enforcement agent, he had a re-sponsibility to find the truth and bring the bad guys to justice. He'd spent a lifetime doing just that. He wanted to tell Bobby Landers what he knew, but he realized that if he did, there would be plenty of questions as to why he was in the Hardisty neighborhood at that hour, questions he hesitated answering. Not that it was any big deal—not to him, anyway. For the better part of six months, he'd been having an affair with Luella Meriweather, widow of the former mayor. The problem was that his kids would throw a fit if they found out, and Lu's would be even worse. It seemed that anyone under forty held with the idea that people his age weren't supposed to think about such things as sex, much less do it, but both he and Lu were single, active and healthy, and it worked for them. Actually, he'd like to marry Lu, but she was afraid that her two daughters would disapprove, so instead of making things legal and aboveboard, they sneaked around like a couple of teenagers.

Micah sighed. Telling what he knew would cause problems, no doubt about it, but not telling would be even worse. He couldn't bear to see Donovan sent up again for something he didn't do. Not Ruby's son.

Ruby Delaney, or Ruby Vaughn, as she'd been thirty-seven years ago, had been his first love. They'd been an item for several months before Micah's dad got a better job in Dallas and moved his family there. Micah, who'd been about to graduate, had gone with them, though leaving Ruby almost killed him. He wrote to her, and she wrote back saying there was no sense in carrying on a long-distance romance, that it was best to end it.

He'd mourned for her for months, and when, a year and a half later, his parents split up and he and his mom and sister moved back to Lewiston, he'd hoped to pick up with Ruby where they'd left off. But he'd come back to town to find that Ruby was married to Hutch and had a young son, Donovan.

He'd been hurt and angry until he'd talked to Opal, Ruby's sister, years later and found out the truth: when he'd left town, Ruby had been pregnant with Donovan. Hutch Delaney, who'd had a crush on her for years, had found out and offered to marry her. To Ruby that alternative had sounded better than welfare and unwed motherhood, so she'd agreed.

She'd come to regret her decision. Even though many of the townsfolk were suspicious of the occasional bruises the Delaneys sported, no one had ever tried to take the kids away from Ruby, and she had never pressed charges against Hutch. Knowing his boy was taking an occasional smacking from Hutch and keeping silent about it was the hardest thing he'd ever done, but Micah was married himself by then, and to say anything would have caused big trouble for a lot of people.

Micah knew Ruby had never really stopped loving him, or he her, but their vows had been important to them, and they had never been unfaithful to their mates. Ruby had died alone, without Micah having had a chance to tell her that a part of him loved her still.

Donovan was a different matter. He might not know the truth about his paternity, but that didn't mean Micah wouldn't do all he could for his son, and that included telling Bobby Landers the truth, no matter if it did mean losing Luella.

Belle was getting restless. She'd been waiting forever, and still no one had come to talk to her. She'd played with her Gameboy until her eyes were crossed and her brain felt fried, and now there was nothing to do. If no one came to talk to her soon, she'd just march out there and demand to speak to someone.

It was just minutes until time for the hearing with Judge Charmichaels when Micah Lawrence walked through the doors of Lewiston's police station. After deciding that he could do nothing but the right thing, he'd gone over to Luella's and told her of his decision. Lu had cried, but she'd agreed. No matter what kind of fallout came from their respective families or the town in general, the authorities needed to know that Donovan was innocent.

"I need to talk to Bobby, Ted," Micah said. "Is he here?"

Ted glanced at the black utilitarian clock hanging on the far wall. "He ought to be here any minute. He, Delaney and Wes Grayson are meeting for the bail hearing."

"That's what I need to talk to him about. There's been a mistake."

"Excuse me."

Both Ted and Micah turned toward the sound of the feminine voice. Lara Hardisty stood a few feet from the desk. She looked rumpled and sleepy and had obviously come from somewhere down the hall. A quick glance at Ted told Micah he was surprised by her sudden appearance.

"Hello, Micah…Ted," she said.

"Hello, Lara."

"Hello, Ms. Hardisty," Ted said. "What can I do for you?"

She feathered her fingers through her hair in a purely feminine gesture. "I came in with some information for Bobby about the Jamerson incident, but

Luke said he'd gone to the hospital to talk to her, but that was—'' she glanced at the silver-tone watch circling her wrist ''—almost three hours ago.''

"Three hours!'' Ted exclaimed with a shake of his head. ''Luke didn't even tell me you were here. I'm sorry, Ms. Hardisty.''

"It's okay,'' she said with a self-conscious smile. "The time passed quickly. I've been sick, and I guess I fell asleep.''

"Well, at least you weren't twiddling your thumbs for three hours,'' Ted said, smiling.

"Did you say you had some information about the Jamerson case?'' Micah asked.

He watched as soft color crept into her cheeks. "Yes. I wanted to come talk to Bobby before he did something stupid like arrest the wrong person.''

A wary expression entered Ted's eyes. ''And who might the wrong person be?''

"Donovan Delaney, of course.''

"I'm sorry, Ms. Hardisty,'' Ted said with shake of his head, ''but Bobby's already arrested Donovan.''

"I didn't have any luck finding Poteet,'' Wes told Donovan just moments before the scheduled hearing. "But the Jamersons did corroborate Lara's story that he's given Lexie a lot of trouble and that he'd been violent with her before. I'm going to keep following that thread until something unravels.''

Donovan flinched visibly at mention of Lara's name. "Does she know?''

"I don't know,'' Wes said. "I tried calling her, but I didn't get an answer.''

There was a buzzing sound, and Bobby strode into the hallway. ''Time to go see the judge, Donnie boy,'' he said as another buzz opened the door to the holding cell.

Donovan and Wes stood. Wes pinned the chief of police with a hostile glare. "At least have the courtesy to call him by his name, *Bobbo*. And leave the cuffs off him. He isn't going anywhere."

Bobby's face turned scarlet with anger. He cuffed Donovan anyway. Without another word they preceded the police chief down the hall to the door leading to the lobby, so they could cross the street to the courthouse situated in the town square. Bobby opened the hall door as Micah Lawrence stepped forward and put a steadying arm around a dark-haired woman. Lara. Wes hesitated. Donovan took a step toward her, and Bobby grabbed his arm.

"No! There's been a terrible mistake," she cried, clinging tightly to Micah's forearm as she spoke to the dispatcher. "Donovan didn't do it. He couldn't have."

The load on Donovan's heart lifted. She'd come. No matter what happened, he could live with it. He glanced at Wes, who smiled.

Bobby shoved them back through the door and growled to Wes to "Keep him here." Then he squared his shoulders and started down the hallway. "What do you mean, he couldn't have?"

Before Lara could answer, a girlish voice cried, "What's the matter with my mom?"

"Belle?" Lara cried, turning toward the sound of her daughter's voice. "What are you doing here?"

Belle? Wes and Donovan exchanged a questioning glance and, by mutual consent, stepped through the door so they could hear better.

Belle came flying down the hall from the opposite direction, putting Lara's back to Donovan. Her arms closed around Belle, and they hugged each other tightly. Then Belle pulled back and looked up at her mother. As she did, she saw Donovan and Wes poised in the doorway down the corridor.

For a moment Donovan thought she would say something, but instead she looked back up at Lara.

"I don't want you to be mad, but I had to come and tell them the truth. What are you doing here?"

"The same thing. You were right, Belle. I have used double standards and you have to tell the truth, no matter what." She turned, and her gaze moved from Bud to Micah and finally to Bobby.

"Donovan Delaney couldn't have hurt Lexie Jamerson last night," she said in a firm voice. "I'm his alibi."

"Beg pardon?" Bobby said, frowning.

Lara's chin lifted in an imperious manner that reminded Donovan of Isabelle, almost as if she dared Bobby to question or doubt what she was about to say. "Donovan couldn't have done that terrible thing to Lexie, because he was at my house. In my bed."

Micah Lawrence's eyes closed, and a look of relief spread across his rugged face.

Bobby opened his mouth to say something, but a commotion at the station's front door stopped him. "What the heck?" he said, instead.

"Stop being so rough, or I'm gonna tear off your head!" came an unfamiliar voice that drew everyone's attention that direction.

"You and what army?" came the terse reply.

"Jett?" Donovan said the name aloud. When he spoke, Lara turned and saw him. She started his way, but before she could take more than two steps, a young man was shoved by an unseen hand into the midst of the gathering crowd, landing in a sprawling heap at Bobby Landers's feet.

Looking like nothing less than a teenage avenging angel, Jett strode into view. "Here's your man, Chief," he said. "This is the scumbag who hurt Lexie, not Donovan."

Chapter Twelve

"No way!" Bobby said, looking from Darren, who was getting up from the floor, to Jett.

"Well, he may not be the culprit," Ted said as Donovan and Wes trekked down the corridor to join the others, "but all these people are here claiming they know for sure that Donovan isn't the guilty party."

"My mom is telling the truth," Belle said, sidling nearer to Lara. "Donovan was with her." Pink tinted her cheeks. "She'd been sick, so I went downstairs to check on her, and I heard them."

Donovan's gaze met Lara's again. Her eyes glistened with tears.

"I can vouch for that," Micah said. "I was in the neighborhood sometime after midnight and saw his Explorer in the driveway."

"What were you doing over there at that time of night?" Bobby asked.

Before Micah could answer, Jett said, "It doesn't matter. Save yourself some time. Darren already admitted he did it."

"I guess this means my client is free to go," Wes said.

Bobby's gaze traveled from face to face. He shook his head. "Not just yet. Let me talk to Darren, and then we'll see."

Jimmy French, who'd gone off duty at least three hours before, came through the doors, clad in old jeans and a T-shirt. He stopped when he saw the gathering at the front desk. "What's going on?"

"They claim we arrested the wrong person," Bobby said. "Jett, here, says Darren confessed. Book him, read him his rights and let him call his parents, will you? Then we'll try to get to the bottom of this."

"B—but I'm off duty, Chief," Jimmy stammered. "I just came to get my reading glasses."

"It won't take long," Bobby said. "For starters, you can take Delaney back to the holding cell."

Looking thoroughly disgusted, Jimmy started to do Bobby's bidding.

"Never mind, Jimmy," Donovan said. "I know the way. I would appreciate it if you'd take these cuffs off." Ted tossed some keys to Jimmy. "Thanks," Donovan said. Without asking anyone's permission, he crossed the space that separated him from Lara. The tears still swimming in her eyes didn't hide her trepidation. He knew she was wondering how her reluctance to come forward sooner had affected their relationship. He was wondering what would have happened if the shoe had been on the other foot. If he'd been forced to tell the truth. Like her, he was unsure where the events that had transpired the past twenty-four hours left them. Nevertheless, he lifted a hand to her cheek and let his fingertips skim the creamy surface. "Thank you."

She gave a little cry and surged against him, wrapping her arms around his neck and kissing him fully on the lips. Donovan would have to have been a much stronger man than he was to push her away.

"See?" Belle said. "I told you."

The sound of her voice brought Donovan back to his senses. He released his hold on Lara, who stepped back and looked up at him with all the love he'd ever hoped to see shining in her eyes. "I'm sorry."

"Hey, this isn't a soap opera," Bobby said. "You two can go at it later."

"Come on, Donovan," Wes said. "I'll walk back with you." To his sister he said, "I'll bring him to your place later."

Lara looked up at him with shining eyes and nodded.

While everyone was giving statements, Ted was on the phone, spreading the news about Lara and Donovan. His wife's baby sister was Rowland Hardisty's nurse—and more, Ted suspected—and as soon as he called his wife, she called her sister, who called Rowland.

So Delaney would be a free man. Free to pursue Lara and worm his way into Belle's life. It was too much. Initially Rowland's objection to Donovan had had more to do with the fact that he was furious about Reed and Sophie and that he couldn't bear the thought of having two Delaneys in the family. He knew that technically Lara wasn't family anymore, but Belle was, and he didn't want Delaney influencing her life.

But Rowland had had plenty of time to think things through since he'd caught Lara and Donovan at Lagniappe's, and the conclusion he'd come to had added fuel to the fire of his dissatisfaction. Though she'd refused to tell anyone who the father of her baby was when she'd married Reed—and Phil had never divulged that bit of information—Rowland was now certain it was Donovan Delaney. Rowland knew his former daughter-in-law well. She wasn't the kind to jump off into a relationship feetfirst, and she and Delaney had gotten too friendly too fast for it to be a recent thing. The only scenario that made sense was that they had meant something to each other in the past.

Well, Belle deserved better than an ex-con for a stepfather, assuming, of course, Delaney would offer marriage. And the children of Lewiston deserved someone with a higher standard from a person who was supposed to be a guiding force in their lives.

Rowland sighed and reached for the phone. It was too bad he had to pop her little bubble of happiness, but it was for the best.

Lara and Belle were allowed to leave after they made formal statements about Donovan being at the house during the time of the rape. They walked to Lara's car, their clasped hands swinging between them. When they reached the car, Lara unlocked it and turned to take Belle in a tight hug.

"I'm very proud of you."

Belle smiled up at her. "And I'm very proud of you."

Lara's smile was tinged with chagrin. "It's really hard to learn your most valuable lessons from kids, but I believe I have. Thanks for making me see that my behavior—my whole thought process—was wrong. We should never put things before people, because things aren't what make us happy. Donovan makes me happy, and we deserve to have a life together, no matter what happened in the past or what people say."

"But you love your job. What if—"

Lara placed a silencing finger over Belle's lips. "I won't. And if it does, it doesn't matter."

"Aunt Isabelle said she could help if things got bad."

Lara rounded the hood of the car. "I don't need Aunt Isabelle."

Belle looked dumbfounded by her mother's new self-confidence. "What are you going to tell Grandpa?"

Lara flashed Belle s mischievous grin. "To mind his own business."

Belle smiled back. "Cool."

Jett told Bobby about his meeting with Darren the day before and about how Darren had come to be in possession of the Delaney Landscape T-shirt. When he'd finished with his statement, he headed for the pay phone and told Cassidy what was happening and that her uncle would be home as soon as a few loose ends were tied up. He heard her give a little sob and relate the news to her mother in a tear-filled voice.

When she got back on the line, he said, "Don't cry, Cass. I'll be there in a little while." Feeling better than he had about himself and the world in general for a

long time, Jett left the station and headed for the Delaney place and Cassidy. He needed to see her. Bad.

Micah supposed that technically he wouldn't have
had to make a statement, what with Lara and her
daughter both saying Donovan was with Lara the night
before, but he was willing to do so anyway. Maybe
because he felt he owed Donovan at least that much.
Maybe because he was tired of the secrecy and sneaking around.

Surprisingly, when the door opened and Jimmy
came into the small room, he told Micah he could go,
that the Poteet kid had confessed, and they wouldn't
need any corroboration of Donovan's whereabouts
from him. Micah left the station both relieved and a
bit disappointed. One thing was for sure, he and Lu
needed to have a serious talk.

Cassidy must have seen him coming, Jett thought as
he pulled to a stop and got out of the truck. She was
waiting on the porch, wearing denim shorts and a
formfitting pullover shirt with a scoop neck and lime-
green-and-orange stripes.

"Hi," she said as he climbed the steps.

"Hi," Jett said, and took her into his arms. He held
on to her tightly, breathing in the scent of her hair and
knowing she and her family were the best things that
had ever happened to him, knowing that he would
spend the rest of his life trying to make up to them for
all they'd given him without even knowing it.

Cassidy pulled back and looked up at him. "Are
you okay?" she asked, confused by the emotion she
sensed running so deeply through him.

He took a finger and looped a lock of hair back behind her ear.

"Oh, look at your hand."

Jett looked down at his knuckles, raw from the blow he'd delivered to Darren. He was still running on adrenaline and hadn't even noticed. "Yeah," he said smiling at her. "I'm okay. Really okay, but when I think about what Darren did to Lexie, I want to rip off his head."

"Tell me what happened," she said, drawing him toward the porch swing. She pulled him down beside her, and he drew her close to his side, just holding her.

Finally he said, "Darren said he did it because Lexie hurt him really bad when she broke up with him—because she wouldn't have sex, by the way. He wanted to hurt her back." Jett shook his head, feeling the unfamiliar sting of tears in his eyes.

For the second time in as many hours, he recounted the story about how Darren got the shirt. Then he told her about the gathering at the station and Bobby Landers's frustration and confusion, finishing with, "Donovan should be here anytime."

Her head resting against his chest, Cassidy shook her head. "He'll go see Lara first. I really hope they can work it out."

"What about us?" Jett asked. "Can we work it out?"

She raised her head and looked at him, smiling a soft smile that did crazy things to his heart. "I don't see me running you off."

"No, but I wouldn't blame you if you did." He brushed a kiss to her forehead. "I'm sorry, Cass."

"For what?"

"For pressing you about…sleeping with me."

"Oh," she said, growing suddenly serious. "That."

"Yeah, that. You're right. No means no, and I should back off and respect that."

"You're being too hard on yourself, Jett. You're a healthy normal teenager—well, barely," she added, knowing he had a birthday coming up. "And so am I. It's no secret that I'm…crazy about you—" that comment brought a tender kiss "—or that I want it as much as you do, but maybe because of what happened to my mom, I know I'm not ready. I couldn't do what she did if I—got pregnant. There's no way I could go off all by myself to a strange town and start a new life. I just couldn't."

"You wouldn't have to," he told her. "I'd take care of you. And that's not just an empty promise to get you to say yes."

"I know. And I believe you would do the right thing if you could, but unexpected things happen. Just ask Lexie or my uncle Donovan."

"I can't argue with that."

"And I still have a lot of school."

"Me, too." Seeing her surprise, he said, "I'm going to Fayetteville in the fall."

"You are?" she asked, her eyes wide.

"Well, don't look so shocked. I may have been a mess up, but that doesn't mean I'm stupid. I was almost a straight-A student, and I did well on my SAT scores."

"But how—"

"How am I going when my mom has three other kids at home and no one to help support them? Donovan helped me fill out some paperwork. I'm getting a grant and a loan."

"But what do you want to do?"

"Don't laugh."

"Never," she said, sketching an *X* over her heart.

"I want to do what Donovan does. It's interesting, challenging and the design part is creative. What more could I want—besides you?"

"Oh, Jett," Cassidy said, her eyes filling with tears.

"Here's the thing," he said brusquely, uncomfortable with the thought of her crying. "We both date while I'm away. After seeing your mom and Mr. Hardisty and Donovan and Miss Lara, I figure if it's the real thing, it can stand the test of time and distance or anything else that might come along."

Cassidy nodded. "If it's the real thing it will last."

Lara and Belle were barely in the door when the phone rang. Thinking it might be Donovan, she snatched it up with a breathless "Hello."

"Lara, this is Lenny Claymore." Lenny Claymore, vice president of the school board.

"Yes, Lenny, what can I do for you?"

"I heard some disturbing news about you and Donovan Delaney a little while ago."

"Really?" Lara asked, already seething. "And what was that?"

"That you are—have been—carrying on an affair with him. And if you are, it's totally unacceptable."

"Oh? Why is that?"

"So it is true?"

"I didn't say that. I only asked why it was unacceptable. We're both single."

"Yes, but he's a *Delaney*. He killed his father."

"In self defense," Lara said. "And he paid for it."

Lara listened to the expected spiel, which was followed by his threat that her job might be in peril, and then she told Lenny that before she allowed them to take her job away for doing what she knew that he himself—and half of the other board members—had done, she'd see them in court.

Blustering about her impertinence, he hung up. The phone rang again almost immediately.

"Hello!" she snapped.

"Lara?" Isabelle said, a wary note in her voice. "Is everything all right?"

"Oh, Aunt Isabelle! I'm sorry I snapped at you, but I just spoke with Lenny Claymore, who heard about me and Donovan, which is, in his words, totally unacceptable. He threatened my job."

"Lenny is generally a peacemaker—not too smart, but not a troublemaker. He only called if someone put him up to it."

"Rowland, I imagine."

"Probably," Isabelle said. "Would you like me to talk to Rowland? I am president of the school board."

"No, thank you, Aunt Isabelle," Lara said. "I'll deal with Rowland myself."

"Good for you," Isabelle murmured. "What do you hear about Donovan?"

"They're letting him go," Lara said. "It was actually quite a circus," she said with a little laugh. "While Belle was with you, I finally came to my senses and went downtown to tell them he was with me. Luke Harrison put me in a little room to wait until Bobby got back, and I fell asleep."

She went on to tell her aunt how, by the time she'd awakened, Donovan had already been arrested and was waiting to get out on bail. She told Isabelle about going out to the front desk and finding Micah Lawrence, who said he had information about the case, talking to the dispatcher.

"And while I was talking to them, trying to tell them Donovan was with me, Belle came out of another room."

"I hope you aren't angry at her, Lara. It was an agonizing decision for her—her mother's job or Donovan going back to jail. But I told her she had to do what she felt was right."

"How could I be angry at her when she did the right thing?"

"So they decided to let him go on the strength of your statement corroborated by Belle?"

"No. About that time, Jett Robbins came bursting through the doors, Darren Poteet by the scruff of the neck. It seems Jett loaned his Delaney Landscape T-shirt to Darren—good grief, was it only yesterday? When he found out about Donovan, he remembered that Darren and Lexie had been having problems and went out to confront him."

"I hate this for Gloria Poteet. She's had such a hard time financially since Mike left her."

"I know."

"As for Jett, I hear he's been in a few minor scrapes with the law, but something about that boy reminds me of Donovan at that age."

"That's what Sophie says."

"So they're releasing Donovan."

"As soon as they tie up a few loose ends, I guess."

"Well," Isabelle said, her voice once again crisp and authoritative, "I'll let you go. I just wanted to see if Belle accomplished her goal and made it home all right."

"Yes, she did, and thanks."

"Marry him, Lara."

"What?"

"Marry Donovan. And soon. Belle will be fine. Unexpected things happen, my dear, as you know only
too well. Time slips away. You'll wake up one morning my age, and wonder why you let one moment go
by without spending it with the man you love. I know,
because I was a fool for separating from Leo that time
I suspected he was fooling around on me."

"Uncle Leo cheated on you?" Lara asked, aghast.

"I could never prove it, but I suspected, and we
separated for a few months. I was miserable, and he
was miserable, but it accomplished something. I never
got so tied up with life that I neglected him and our
marriage, and I never ever took him for granted
again."

Lara, who'd never imagined Isabelle's marriage to
be anything but perfect was stunned by this revelation.

"I look back, and I wish I could have all those lost
days and nights," Isabelle said, her voice thoughtful.
"Even though being in the same room with him in-
furiated me at the time, if I hadn't kicked him out, I'd
have at least had him near me. Seize the day, Lara.
We aren't promised tomorrow."

Lara thought about Isabelle's confession as she fixed
sandwiches for herself and Belle and waited to hear
from Donovan. Isabelle was right. Life was short and
uncertain. Like Reed and Sophie, she and Donovan
were lucky to have a second chance. It made no sense
to wait when they'd already waited more than seventeen years to be together. They loved each other, and
that love would help them get through any hard times
that might crop up in the future, including any problems Rowland might cause with her job.

Rowland. She might as well deal with him now as later. Checking the kitchen clock, she decided he should be at home having dinner before making his evening rounds at the hospital.

She punched in the number, and he answered on the second ring.

"This is Lara," she said without preamble. "We need to talk."

"About?" he asked.

"About your campaign to boot me out of my position as principal."

"I don't know what you're talking about," he said smoothly.

"Of course you do," Lara snapped. "You've already threatened me, and now you're starting to put other board members up to calling me—the same board members who were against my getting the job in the first place."

"Settle down, Lara, and think this through like a rational adult."

"I am settled down, and I am a rational adult who has thought it through. In case you haven't heard, they're letting Donovan go. He didn't do it, which everyone should have known if they hadn't been so narrow-minded and blinded by the fact that he's a Delaney. Donovan is a good man, Rowland, and I will continue to see him. And if he wants me, I'm going to marry him."

"I won't have an ex-con as my granddaughter's stepfather," Rowland said, his voice growing hard.

"And what do you plan to do about it?"

"I'll fight you in court."

Lara laughed, but she trembled with anger. "Fight me in court? A custody battle? May I remind you of two things. First, even though you're a wealthy man, the combined Grayson resources make you look like a pauper. Second, why would any judge alive take a child away from her divorced mother who was having an affair to give her to a married man who's having an affair with his nurse?''

"Why, you—"

"What's the matter, Rowland? Did you actually think no one knew about you and Trudy? The whole town knows, including Celeste."

For once Rowland had no comment.

"So here's what I'm willing to do," Lara said, her stomach churning. "You stop with your vendetta against Donovan and stop threatening my job, and I'll let you see Belle. If you don't, well, you'll have to be satisfied seeing her at family gatherings, and you and the school board will see me in court."

"You can't do that!" he said, finding his voice once more.

"Hide and watch me," Lara said. "That's the deal. Take it or leave it."

"You'd really stop Belle from seeing me?"

"In a heartbeat. And you know what the really sad thing is? She adores her grandmother, but I have to *make* her spend time with *you*."

She heard his surprised gasp.

"It takes more than spending money on a child to win love and respect, Rowland. They can spot a fake at a hundred paces. Belle sees how you treat other people, her new sister included, and it bothers her. Maybe you should stop trying to impress the world with your skill as a surgeon and concentrate on your people skills a bit more."

* * *

"Where to?" Wes asked Donovan when the police released him. "Your place or Lara's?"

Donovan glanced at his watch. All the florists' shops were closed. "Take me to Isabelle's."

"Isabelle's?" Wes said. "Why?"

"I need some flowers."

Wes grinned. "Sure."

He drove Donovan to Isabelle's, who insisted on their having a bite of dinner with her. They agreed, even though Wes knew Donovan must be chomping at the bit to get to Lara. Then Wes and Isabelle walked along with Donovan as he wandered through Isabelle's garden with a basket and some shears, stopping every now and then to ask her what certain flowers represented in the language of flowers.

When Wes looked askance at her, she said, "He's going to make a tussie-mussie. The lamb's ear is for support. The feverfew is for health. The lemon balm is supposed to drive away heaviness of mind, and the bachelor's buttons and yarrow are for health and healing."

When Donovan had a nice handful of flowers and leaves, he went into Isabelle's potting shed and began to cut stems and place the flowers in a small, compact, incredibly beautiful bouquet that he wrapped with a wet paper towel, cling wrap and florist's tape.

When he finished, he and Wes kissed Isabelle on the cheek and thanked her for dinner and the flowers. Donovan turned to Wes. "Take me to the hospital."

"The hospital?"

"Yeah. I want to go see Lexie Jamerson, and then you can take me to Lara's."

* * *

Lara was waiting by the window and ran out the front door as soon as Wes pulled the roadster convertible into the driveway. Donovan was barely out of the car when she flew into his arms. He kissed her with a hunger that bordered on desperation and spoke volumes about his earlier fears.

"What took you so long?" she asked.

"I wanted to go visit the Jamersons and see Lexie," he said. "I wanted to take her some flowers to cheer her up, but all the shops were closed, so Wes drove me out to Isabelle's. She insisted we have dinner with her."

Any man who'd just been released from jail, whose first thought was of another person, had to be a very special man, Lara thought, gazing up at him with something closely akin to awe. Despite all he'd been through there was an inherent gentleness in Donovan Delaney, and she knew she was very lucky to be loved by him.

"That was incredibly thoughtful of you."

He shrugged, dismissing the praise and the subject. "Thanks for what you did," he said again.

"You shouldn't thank me. You should be furious with me. If I'd spoken up sooner, you wouldn't have had to spend even an hour in that terrible place."

"No harm done," he said, brushing her hair away from her face with a gentle hand.

"Really?" She gazed up at him with troubled eyes. He knew he was talking about the situation in general, but her question referred specifically to their relationship.

"Really. All that matters is that you came."

Wes cleared his throat. "I hate to interrupt this touching scene, but if the two of you don't need me for anything else, I'll go on home."

Lara and Donovan smiled at him. "I'll drive him home later," she said.

"Great. I'll call you in a day or two." He put the roadster in gear and started to back out the driveway.

"Hey!" Donovan called as the car backed onto the street. "Send me a bill, and I'll write you a check."

Wes waved away the idea. "Consider it a wedding gift."

They watched as he turned the corner and disappeared.

"Is there going to be a wedding?" Lara asked sliding her arms around his waist and looking up at him. "Or do you still want to tie yourself to a wishy-washy woman with no backbone?"

Donovan smiled. "I still want to marry a woman who's worked hard to make a place for herself, who thinks things through and doesn't make rash decisions, and who does the right thing no matter what."

Lara gazed up at him through a film of tears. "I don't deserve you, but if that's a proposal, the answer is yes. As soon as possible."

Even though he must have suspected what her answer would be, Donovan looked surprised. "Soon? Like when?"

"As soon as we can get a license and find a justice of the peace."

"You don't want a big shindig like Reed and Sophie?"

"No. I want to wake up with you in my bed every day and fall asleep with you holding me every night," she said, a solitary tear slipping free. She lifted a hand to his cheek, her thumb resting at the corner of his mouth. "I want to learn about propagation and cultivars and pruning. I want to have your baby."

She saw the tears in Donovan's eyes before he tightened his hold on her and lowered his head for a kiss.

"I guess you know you're making a spectacle of yourselves. If you want to make out, at least go out back."

The comment caused Donovan and Lara to jump apart guiltily. Belle stood a few feet from them, a tray with three glasses of milk and three various snack cake packages on it.

Donovan smiled at her. "You're right. We don't want the neighbors talking." He gestured toward the tray.

"What's that?"

"I thought we could celebrate. You know, for justice being served. And for an engagement?" The last was asked as a question as she looked from Donovan to Lara.

"Yes," Donovan said. "Definitely an engagement. But a very short one. Like days. Is that okay with you?"

"Yeah," Belle said, much to Lara's relief. "That's okay with me. Now follow me. We'll have our celebration out by the pool," she said in an imperious voice that sounded remarkably like Isabelle.

Dutifully, casting smiles at each other, Donovan and Lara followed. They were halfway to the house when Belle stopped and turned to them. "And about this baby thing. Does this mean I have to baby-sit and change yucky diapers and get thrown up on?"

"We're all three in this marriage together," Lara said, "so yes."

Belle grinned broadly. "Cool."

* * * * *

#1 *New York Times* bestselling author

NORA ROBERTS

brings you more of the loyal and loving,
tempestuous and tantalizing Stanislaski family.

Coming in February 2001

The Stanislaski Sisters

Natasha and Rachel

Though raised in the Old World traditions of their
family, fiery Natasha Stanislaski and cool, classy
Rachel Stanislaski are ready for a *new* world of love....

And also available in February 2001 from
Silhouette Special Edition, the newest book in the
heartwarming Stanislaski saga

CONSIDERING KATE

Natasha and Spencer Kimball's daughter Kate turns her
back on old dreams and returns to her hometown, where
she finds the *man* of her dreams.

Available at your favorite retail outlet.

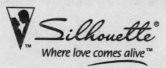

Where love comes alive™

Coming in January 2001 from Silhouette Books...

ChildFinders, Inc.:
AN UNCOMMON HERO
by
MARIE FERRARELLA

the latest installment of
this bestselling author's popular miniseries.

The assignment seemed straightforward: track down the woman who
had stolen a boy and return him to his father. But ChildFinders, Inc.
had been duped, and Ben Underwood soon discovered that nothing
about the case was as it seemed. Gina Wassel, the supposed kidnapper,
was everything Ben had dreamed of in a woman, and suddenly he had
to untangle the truth from the lies—before it was too late.

Available at your favorite retail outlet.

Silhouette®

Where love comes alive™

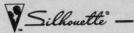

Silhouette —

where love comes alive—online...

eHARLEQUIN.com

your romantic
books

- ♥ **Shop online!** Visit Shop eHarlequin and discover a wide selection of new releases and classic favorites at great discounted prices.

- ♥ **Read** our daily and weekly Internet exclusive serials, and participate in our interactive novel in the reading room.

- ♥ **Ever dreamed of being a writer?** Enter your chapter for a chance to become a featured author in our Writing Round Robin novel.

● ● ● ● ● ● ●

your romantic
life

- ♥ **Check out** our feature articles on dating, flirting and other important romance topics and get your daily love dose with tips on how to keep the romance alive every day.

● ● ● ● ● ● ●

your
community

- ♥ **Have a Heart-to-Heart** with other members about the latest books and meet your favorite authors.

- ♥ **Discuss** your romantic dilemma in the Tales from the Heart message board.

your romantic
escapes

- ♥ **Learn** what the stars have in store for you with our daily Passionscopes and weekly Erotiscopes.

- ♥ **Get** the latest scoop on your favorite royals in Royal Romance.

Silhouette®

CMN1200

SPECIAL EDITION